DEATH FOR LIFE

The big man with red hair looked down at the man he had felled with a savage short right. Then he turned to the barkeep and said, "Pitcher of water, please."

Behind him there was a soft scrape of metal against leather. He whirled. The figure on the floor had turned over, and his sixgun had already cleared the holster. The big man's answering draw had the speed of leaping flame and the ivory-gripped Colt seemed to fire while still in motion.

"Jesus," the barkeep breathed as he leaned over to look at the gaping red hole in the sprawled figure's chest. "That was some shooting. You got a name?"

"Canyon O'Grady," the big man said.

"That was the fastest draw I ever saw, mister," the barkeep persisted.

Canyon smiled at the unsaid question. "I'm no gunhand. But being fast comes in handy if you like living, and I do."

CANYON O'GRADY

4

SHADOW GUNS

by

Jon Sharpe

A SIGNET BOOK

NEW AMERICAN LIBRARY

A DIVISION OF PENGUIN BOOKS USA INC.

NAL BOOKS ARE AVAILABLE AT QUANTITY DISCOUNTS WHEN USED
TO PROMOTE PRODUCTS OR SERVICES. FOR INFORMATION PLEASE
WRITE TO PREMIUM MARKETING DIVISION, NEW AMERICAN
LIBRARY, 1633 BROADWAY, NEW YORK, NEW YORK 10019.

The first chapter of this book previously appeared in *Machine Gun
Madness*, the third volume in this series.

SIGNET TRADEMARK REG. U.S. PAT OFF. AND FOREIGN COUNTRIES
REGISTERED TRADEMARK—MARCA REGISTRADA
HECHO EN DRESDEN, TN, U.S.A.

SIGNET, SIGNET CLASSIC, MENTOR, ONYX, PLUME,
MERIDIAN and NAL BOOKS are published by New American
Library, a division of Penguin Books USA Inc., 1633 Broadway,
New York, New York 10019

First Printing, November, 1989

1 2 3 4 5 6 7 8 9

PRINTED IN THE UNITED STATES OF AMERICA

Canyon O'Grady

His was a heritage of blackguards and poets, fighters and lovers, men who could draw a pistol and bed a lass with the same ease.

Freedom was a cry seared into Canyon O'Grady, justice a banner of the heart.

With the great wave of those who fled to America, the new land of hope and heartbreak, solace and savagery, he came to ride the untamed wildness of the Old West.

With a smile or a sixgun, Canyon O'Grady became a name feared by some and welcomed by others but remembered by all . . .

*Missouri, 1859, west of a
Thousand Hills, a state half-free
and half-slave, a land where hate
was only a stepping-stone to power . . .*

1

"She'll be getting herself killed," the big red-haired man muttered aloud. "And she's too lovely for that," he added, his clear blue eyes looking down at the scene at the foot of the hill. The young woman rode her horse full out as she chased the big bay, the lariat in her hand. She had made two tries to rope the running horse from a half-dozen yards behind, and he'd winced each time.

He saw that she was trying again, and he sent his own horse downhill while his eyes stayed riveted on the racing bay. The horse ran in a huge circle as the girl pursued. It wasn't a wild horse, not with the smooth, well-groomed condition of its coat. But it was worse than a wild horse, the big man grunted, it was a powerful animal crazed with fear or hate, filled with emotions more directed than that of a wild horse.

The big man had almost reached the bottom of the hill when he saw the young woman swirling the lariat as she prepared to throw it again. She'd keep herself alive if she missed again, he muttered inwardly, but he saw her send the lariat through the air. This time she didn't miss, the loop settling over the horse's neck, and she immediately pulled her own mount to a halt. She started to yank back on the lariat and the flame-haired man opened his mouth to shout, but it was too late. His lips pulled back in a grimace as he saw her fly from her saddle headfirst and slam into the ground. The lasso flew from her hands as she hit, and the big bay skidded to a halt, then turned and started back toward her, its nostrils flared and ears laid back.

The red-haired man swerved his horse to charge forward just as the big bay came to a halt and reared up on its hind legs. Shouting at the top of his voice, he raced between the young woman on the ground and the bay's flailing hooves. The angry horse took a step backward, and its sharp-edged hooves struck into the ground. But, though snorting in anger, it stayed still. He'd try again, the big flame-haired man knew by the wild fury in his eyes. A quick glance at the girl saw her pushing herself to her feet, her forehead smudged with dirt. It didn't take away from the fine looks of her, he noted.

"Can you run?" he called out, and she nodded. "Get over to that hickory over there," he said.

"Can you get it?" she asked as she started to move toward the tree.

"I'll try, but nobody can do it the way you did," he snapped. He heard the big bay's snort of anger and turned his attention back to the horse. The bay started to back up, then it turned, and the big man yanked his lariat from the lariat strap, twirling it in the air even before he began to chase after the bay. He spurred his own, bronze-hued horse into a gallop, caught up to the bay, and saw the runaway mount immediately begin to veer away in a wide circle. But the horse and rider stayed with him, and the bay shortened the diameter of the circle. The red-haired man edged his own mount up another few feet, almost against the runaway bay's flank, and flung the lariat in a short, accurate toss that sent the loop descending over the other horse's neck.

But he made no attempt to skid to a halt and pull back on the lariat. Instead, he raced almost alongside the bay, pulling the lariat in a slow, steady pressure until the other horse began to slow. He tightened the lariat again, using the power and weight of his own horse to help pull back on the rope. Finally, as the bay completed the circle, it began to slow. It still resisted, tried to shake the rope loose, but the slow, steady pressure on the rope remained and it finally broke into a trot and then a walk. His captor brought it into a tighter circle, then steered the horse beside a tree where the young woman waited. He wrapped the lariat around a low branch and secured the horse in place before he swung from the saddle.

"That was extraordinary," the young woman said. "I guess I went about it all wrong. I've never had to do that before."

"Let's just say you're not ready to take up the

wrangler's life yet.'' The big, flame-haired man smiled. ''You can't rope him to a stop from way back where you were. Nobody's strong enough for that.''

''So I found out,'' she said ruefully.

''You have to go with it, slow it down with a steady pressure or you'll have your arms pulled out of their sockets or break your neck when you go flying,'' he said. ''And we wouldn't want that,'' he added as he let his eyes survey the young woman with slow deliberateness. He took in a straight, thin nose, delicately flared, thin black eyebrows, a slender body with breasts that curved in a lovely, long line under a pale-yellow shirt, and he gave voice to the rest of what he saw. ''Hair black as a raven's wing, eyes to match and skin white as Egyptian alabaster,'' he murmured.

The thin black eyebrows arched and a smile edged her lips. ''A poet with a lilt in his voice and a wrangler of rare skill,'' she said. ''An unlikely combination indeed.''

''Unlikely and untrue, seeing as I can't own up to either.'' The big man laughed and saw her take in the red of his hair, the roguish cast of his face, and the snapping blue of his eyes.

''You can own up to a name, I presume,'' she said, cool amusement in her almost black eyes. Amusement and interest, he corrected himself.

''Indeed. It's Canyon O'Grady at your service,'' he said with a half-bow.

Her smile became a soft laugh. ''A most unusual name for a most unusual man, I suspect,'' she said. "I'm Carla Gannet."

Canyon O'Grady let his gracious smile mask the surprise that flashed through him. He accepted her remark with a shrug and turned to look at the big bay again. It was a splendid piece of horseflesh, with a deep chest, strong rump, and well-placed neck. It was a horse made for powerful running. But its ears were still laid back, with the wildness still in its eyes. Carla Gannet brought her tall, slender form alongside Canyon to gaze at the horse.

"It's one of my father's horses, but there's only one man who can handle and ride him. I took it out to try to work with it, a foolish thing on my part. It bolted from the exercise ring, I chased it and you know the rest," Carla said. "It's a mean horse, real bad-tempered. It hates all people except for Owen."

"I take it Owen's the one man that handles it," Canyon said.

"Yes, Owen Dunstan. He's a family friend and one of my gentlemen callers," Carla said.

"A special one?" Canyon smiled.

"Perhaps. He thinks so," she replied.

Canyon stepped closer to the horse and studied the animal for a few minutes in silence. The horse stepped backward at once, its eyes rolling back in its head and its ears going flat. Yet it took a step forward, a challenging movement. Canyon moved back and the horse took another step forward.

"It's been made mean," Canyon said, turning to the young woman.

Her thin, black eyebrows lowered, as a furrow crossed the smoothness of her alabaster brow. "How can you say that?"

"I've seen enough real mean actors," Canyon said. "They've a different kind of eye, and they're ready to charge and trample you anytime they get the chance. Your bay doesn't have that eye. And I've seen wild horses you can't ever really tame. They have their own special brand of wildness, a kind of raging pride they never lose. You can always see that in them. This horse isn't any of those. He's been handled wrong, made to obey instead of to want to obey."

Carla Gannet's black eyes danced with a combination of amusement and admiration as she studied the big, flame-haired man. "You know your horses, Canyon O'Grady," she said. "But Owen wouldn't like hearing that."

"Too bad for Owen," Canyon grunted coldly.

She smiled as she turned to look at Canyon O'Grady's magnificent palomino, taking in the horse with a practised eye. "This is the most beautiful palomino I've ever seen," she said. "I imagine he's a very special horse."

"He is," Canyon agreed blandly, and rubbed a hand across the pale-bronze fur and blond mane.

"What do you call him?" Carla Gannet asked.

"Cormac," Canyon said.

The faint smile touched her lips again. "Another unusual name, I might have expected as much," she said.

"King Cormac was one of the four great legendary Irish kings," Canyon explained.

The young woman's smile stayed as she peered at the big, red-haired man with amused appraisal. "Who are you, Canyon O'Grady?"

"A wanderer, a searcher, a tinker, a mender of whatever needs mending." Canyon smiled. "Runaway horses or runaway hearts."

"And a man quicker with words than answers." She laughed, a velvety sound.

"Never," he said in mock protest, and his attention turned to the distance where a horse and rider raced toward them.

"Owen," Carla Gannet said.

Canyon watched the rider grow larger, slow to a halt, and leap to the ground. He took in a tall man wearing a loose-sleeved, dark shirt open at the neck, carefully combed hair, and a handsome face, but one that wore arrogance in it. He noted good shoulders, a flat figure with narrow-hipped grace.

Owen Dunstan's eyes went directly to the young woman as he faced her, a riding crop in his right hand and anger in his face. "Dammit, Carla, you'd no right taking it out of the stall," he said. "You know I'm the only one who can handle it."

"It's Daddy's horse," Carla returned. "I thought the exercise would do it good. It hasn't been out for two days."

"You'd no right, especially two days before the meet," Owen Dunstan repeated angrily.

"My mistake," Carla said.

Canyon saw that Owen Dunstan ingored him as a king ignores a stable boy and he watched in silence as the man turned to look at the big bay. "You were very lucky, Carla. I don't know how you managed to get it back," Dunstan said to the young woman.

"I didn't. This man did," Carla said, gesturing to Canyon.

Dunstan turned to look directly at the big red-haired man for the first time, a faint arch of his eyebrows his only acknowledgment. "I see," Owen Dunstan said. "Well, if you come back with me, I'll see that you're paid for your trouble."

Canyon saw that the arrogance in the man's face was but a reflection of his character. "Do you work at being gratuitous or does it just come naturally to you, old boy?" he said.

He watched Owen Dunstan take a moment to absorb the answer, and enjoyed the touch of surprise that came into the man's face. "I don't like your tone," Dunstan snapped.

"That makes us even," Canyon answered.

"People don't talk to me in that tone, mister."

"Then look at this as a refreshing change," Canyon replied.

Owen was too arrogant to detect the steel behind the smile. He stepped forward, the riding crop raised in one hand. "Perhaps you need a lesson in manners."

Canyon eyed the riding crop with almost

amused tolerance. "The last man who raised one of those to me has never been able to take a drink without pain since," Canyon said, watching Dunstan's face grow florid. But the man had suddenly taken notice of the danger in the big man's eyes, and he lowered the riding crop.

"Stop it this minute, Owen," Carla Gannet's voice interrupted. "This man saved me and he saved your horse. You owe him an apology."

Dunstan spun on her. "You apologize to him. This has all been your fault, Carla," he growled. He strode to the horse, untied it, and swung onto the animal's back. He rode off at a fast trot, not looking back and pulling the second horse along with him.

Canyon saw the young woman turn to him. "I'm sorry," she said. "Good manners desert him when he's upset."

"And you're good at making excuses for him," Canyon remarked. "He doesn't seem worth it."

"He's a product of his background, his life-style. That's just the kind of thinking and behavior that goes with it. But, then, isn't that what we all are?"

"Indeed, only most of us aren't bred into arrogance," Canyon answered.

"Let's forget Owen," she said. "I'm very grateful to you and I'd like to know a lot more about Canyon O'Grady. This is a festive week around these parts. Daddy's having a big party tomorrow night at our place. Please come. I'm sure he'll want to thank you for saving his daughter's neck."

"I've no fancy clothes," Canyon demurred.

"Come as you are. You'll be my guest," she said, and her hand rested against his arm.

"Now, how could I turn down being the guest of the most beautiful woman that will be there?" Canyon laughed.

"Then I'll see you tomorrow night at the house. Ask anybody where it is," she said, and he watched the curve of her breasts sway beautifully as she pulled herself onto her horse. She held her hand out and he took it, pressing the soft smoothness of it against his lips. Her smile held the hint of promise in the soft corners of her mouth. "I'll be looking for you, Canyon O'Grady," she said, putting the horse into a trot.

He watched her become a small and distant figure riding across the low hills. "Carla Gannet," he murmured aloud to himself while a smile touched his lips. A stroke of luck, entirely unexpected, he reflected. And he wouldn't be turning his back on it.

The day hadn't been a total loss. He had done a good deed, met a beautiful woman, and made an enemy. Life was a thing of balances, and his were about to grow more precarious. But then, that's what had brought him to this state called Missouri.

The Indians had named it the place of people of the big canoes. The white man had made it a place of big hopes and big heartaches, a land that seethed with a thousand fires of the spirit. Maybe he could put one out. Or make another burn more brightly. Time would tell, and Carla Gannet was a lovely place to start.

2

The low gentle hills were made for idle riding, Canyon decided, and there was enough of the day left to explore the land. Besides, the meeting with his contact wasn't until night, so he sent the palomino forward at a walk as he scanned the land. Familiarity breeds contempt was an old saying that didn't apply to learning a terrain. "Familiarity breeds reassurance," he murmured, and he made a mental map as he rode.

The day had begun to drift into dusk when he paused atop a hillock and looked down at the buildings and corrals a few hundred yards away. He took in a modest ranch house, two large stables, and a barn. A half-dozen neat corrals with freshly painted fences surrounded the buildings.

He was still surveying the spread when he saw the horsemen come over the low rise, and the furrow dug into his brow at once. "Trouble," he muttered. He knew it was there, just in the way they were riding, hard and bunched tightly together. His sixth sense was at work, and he knew the reality of intuition too well to ignore it as some did.

He moved out of sight beneath the large, shallow lobed leaves of a black maple and watched the riders near the ranch. He counted six of them, and saw them suddenly swerve as they came abreast of the buildings. As they raced at the ranch, he saw that some carried rifles and others clublike sticks, bulbous at one end. Two reined up in front of the main house and leapt from their horses while the other four spread out. Suddenly he saw the clublike sticks begin to blaze at one end.

"By god," Canyon gasped as the four riders wheeled their horses in a tight circle and tossed the blazing torches against both stable doors and the half-open wide doors of the barn. "They're setting fire to the place," Canyon muttered in astonishment.

O'Grady brought his hand down hard on the palomino's rump and the powerful horse shot forward into a full gallop. He reached the ranch to see the barn door already ablaze as hay scattered on the floor caught fire instantly. The two closed stable doors were beginning to burn, and two of the men disappeared into the house.

Canyon, the big, ivory-gripped Army model Colt in his hand, yelled curses at the remaining four men. They turned to come at him, raising their rifles, but the Colt erupted in a hail of bullets. Not a wild, scatter-shot barrage, but shots fired with a speed that almost defied their accuracy. Three of the torch-bearing riders fell from their horses almost simultaneously.

The fourth one got a shot off, but it was fired in wild haste and he never had the chance to fire another as the ivory-gripped Colt exploded again. The man clutched at his forehead, an automatic reaction as he fell with the top of his head blown away.

Canyon was swinging from the saddle when he saw the other two attackers come from the house dragging a white-haired figure with them. ''Let him go,'' Canyon shouted, and the men halted. They stared at the four figures scattered on the ground and turned to the big red-head. They dropped the white-haired figure as they dived in opposite directions and drew their guns. Canyon dropped and rolled to avoid being caught in the cross fire. He kept rolling and came against a long, narrow water trough as bullets continued to kick up dirt only inches from him. He swore silently as he saw the barn door being quickly engulfed in flames. He came up on one knee behind the end of the trough just in time to see the two men leap up and race for their horses.

He drew a bead on one and fired. The man did a stumbling, kicking step as he continued forward until he fell onto his face. The last one had reached his horse and started to race away, his figure hunched low in the saddle. But Canyon noted that he wore a dark buckskin jacket with the fringes dyed a lighter brown. Canyon also noticed that the man's horse had two white rear feet.

O'Grady rose and ran to the white-haired figure on the ground, the crackle of flame and the smell of smoke filling the air now. The sound of horses snorting and neighing in fear could be heard inside the stables. The white-haired man tried to rise onto one elbow, and Canyon saw the red gash across his forehead. He turned away from the man, who still tried to gather himself, pain clear in a lined, crinkly face.

Canyon ran to the barn, where flames were moving up the sides of the wide door with quickening intensity. There was still a narrow section untouched, and the door stood partly ajar. O'Grady raced into the barn and felt the hot breath of the fire. The straw on the barn floor near the door was burning, each piece catching another on fire, and the deep mewing of cows formed a bass obbligato to the crackling sound of the flaming door.

But he spotted the four fire pails at the head of the first stall, two filled with water, two with sand. He snapped up a pail of sand first and flung the contents over the floor in a wide, sweeping motion. It quickly doused the straw burning just inside the door. He took the other three pails, two in one hand, one in the other, and ducked out of the door. He ran past the flames that blew hot against his face, flung the contents of each pail against the outside of the door, and saw the instant billow of smoke rise. But he realized it would only slow the fire for a few minutes, unless he could continue the attack.

The two stable doors, made of stronger and newer wood, hadn't burst into flame yet, but he saw the thin red lines crawling across their cracks and knew it was but minutes before they'd also burst into flame.

The wavering call broke into his grim thoughts, and he turned to find the white-haired figure leaning against a well a dozen feet away. "Over here," the man rasped, and Canyon raced for the well, scooping up the empty pails without breaking stride. The sound of horses neighing in panic had grown louder and he reached the well as the elderly man pulled a bucket up, his face mirroring the effort, and Canyon filled one pail and then another.

As the old man lowered the bucket again, Canyon raced away. When he reached the buildings, he tossed the water against one of the stable doors and then the other. Again, smoke rose from where the tendrils of flame had been crossing the doors, and Canyon raced back to the well, where the other two pails were filled and waiting. The barn door had erupted into leaping, broad flames again.

Canyon flung both pails of water against it, saw the flames shrink, then edge back around the front of the door. Once again he returned to the well, took the two pails, and ran back to the barn. The flames were higher than his head now, feeding hungrily on untouched wood. He flung the water against them and again saw only a moment's respite. He couldn't throw enough water on the burning doors single-handedly, he realized. The flames rushed upward every time he ran to get another set of pails, and he cursed as his eye swept the ground and spotted the toolshed a half-dozen yards away.

He ran toward it and felt the heat of the barn door follow him as the fire began to engulf it from top to bottom. The flame cast an orange glow through the gathering dusk as he pulled the door of the shed open and saw the long-handled axes inside among the other tools. He yanked the nearest one out and charged back to the barn, where he began to frantically chop the wide door at the hinges where the flames hadn't reached yet. Out of the corner of his eye he saw the white-haired man half-crawling, half-stumbling toward him with another pail of water. But Canyon sunk the ax into the wood, tore at it, and felt it splinter under his blows. The only chance was to rip the door down before the flames swept from it to the rest of the barn.

He turned his face away from the blast of heat that came from the leaping flames. But he kept the ax tearing into the doorframe at the hinges, and he saw that the white-haired man had collapsed on the ground near the well. A burst of flame came at Canyon, making him stop and fall back for an instant, but he returned to the door as soon as the flames curled upward and away from him. He kept chopping, and suddenly felt the top hinge give way. He leapt backward as the door fell out and toward him. The weight of it tore the bottom hinge loose, and the door collapsed on the ground with a shower of sparks and flame. But it was no longer attached to the as-yet-untouched wood of the rest of the barn.

Canyon turned and raced toward the nearest of the stable doors. The thin lines of red had become leaping tongues of fire as he began to chop at the doorframe. He was gouging out big chunks of the wood when he heard the hoofbeats, and out of the corner of one eye, he glimpsed the lone rider racing out of the fast-deepening dusk.

Canyon sank the ax deep into the wood at the edge of the door and saw the horse skid to a halt and the rider leap off, a girl's round, smooth cheeks under short brown hair. He saw the rifle in her hands as she hit the ground. He started to protest when she spun and aimed at him. But decided there was no time and he flung himself to the ground, the ax falling from his hand.

Two shots slammed into the burning stable door just over his head. "No, dammit. Hold it, hold it," he shouted.

"Bastards. Rotten, stinking bastards," the girl shouted, a waver in her voice, and Canyon saw another shot slam into the ground near his head.

"No, Glenda, no," a voice cut in, and Canyon saw the white-haired figure on one knee, waving an arm at the girl.

Canyon raised his head and saw her running toward the old man; she dropped to her knees beside him. Canyon rose, picked up the ax and began chopping at the frame of the door again. He had just torn away the hinge when the small-ish figure came alongside him and tossed the pail of water on the flames.

"I'm sorry," she breathed. "We'll talk later." She turned and started to run for the well as the door came loose and fell to the ground.

Canyon scooped up two of the pails and ran after her. He caught up to her at the well and he took in a round-cheeked face, pretty, with a very determined chin, a short nose, and brown eyes. It was a face that held an aggressive, tomboy quality in it. She didn't try to talk as he drew the water from the well and returned to the stable door that still burned.

They worked together, dousing the door with two buckets of water at once. After two more trips to the well, the fire sputtered out, and all that remained was a soaked, charred object with smoke rising from its sides.

Canyon slumped over, took a deep breath, and saw the young woman helping the white-haired man to sit down at the steps of the main house. He straightened, stretched, and heard the still-frightened horses from inside the stables as he walked to where the young woman knelt beside the old man.

"I never got a chance to get my rifle," Canyon heard the man say. "They just came in and conked me with the barrel of a six-gun."

"I'll help you in and wash that cut clean," the young woman said.

"No, see to the horses. Let them out. That'll calm them down," the old man said, and pushed to his feet. His glance went to Fargo. "They'd have killed me except for that feller there," he said. "He saved me, saved everything you've got here, Glenda."

He slowly turned to enter the house and the young woman came to where Fargo waited. She had a compact, firm figure, a little short-legged, but with high, full breasts. She had a way of walking that matched the pretty pugnaciousness in her face, not quite a swagger but close enough to one. "I can't talk now. I've too much to do. I can't even thank you properly. Can you come back tomorrow? Please,'' she added in emphasis.

"I'll do that. Got some questions of my own," Fargo said. "One of them got away, but I don't expect he'll be back."

She nodded. "Tomorrow. We'll talk then," she said and her hand pressed his arm. "Meanwhile, thank you for what you did, and I'm sorry I came in firing at you. I thought you were one of them."

"It ended all right. That's what counts," Canyon replied. He watched her turn and stride toward the nearest stable, saw a compact, very round little rear that filled the riding britches. He swung onto the palomino and rode away, casting a glance back through the night. He saw the dark shapes race out into corrals. It seemed to be his day for good deeds, he reflected as he rode slowly through the night. But it was the first one that promised rewards. Perhaps more than he had a right to expect, but he couldn't stop thinking about how Carla Gannet had looked at him. Perhaps she would be a most pleasant road to his goal. Or a trap, he grunted harshly. She was lovely enough to be either and he'd best not be forgetting that, he reminded himself.

3

Canyon pushed away further pleasant musings and pointed the palomino toward the town that called itself Dry Corn. He had already ridden through it a day ago, had taken the measure of the town, and gone on. Its name fit. It was a treeless town with dry-dust streets and weathered, sun-baked buildings. But it boasted a bank and a dry-goods store along with the usual dance-hall saloon, the Dry Corn Kitten. And now it was time to return to the town, to the saloon. His contact was to meet him there. The exact night had been left open, seeing that it was certain only that he'd arrive sometime during the week. Perhaps the contact would be there tonight, but if not, he'd visit the Dry Corn Kitten as often as it took.

The town was still and dark when he rode in, the only sound the murmur of voices coming from the saloon, a beacon of light in the night. Canyon had just tethered the palomino to the hitching post when he saw the horse a few feet away, its coat still glistening with lather, but it was the two white feet he spotted first and he strode to the saloon with a glare in his eyes.

Canyon O'Grady pushed into the dance-hall saloon, his quick glance taking in an ordinary-enough place with a dozen round tables along the sides, a sawdust-covered dance floor, and a bar against one wall. He spotted the man at once, the dark buckskin jacket with the fringes dyed a lighter tone was almost too easy to find. He started toward the bar and one of the dance-hall girls stepped into his path. She wore a tight, bare-shouldered frock and a false, mechanical smile, and he brushed past her before she could begin her well-rehearsed approach. He watched the man in the buckskin jacket down his drink in short, fast gulps and wipe his lips with the back of his hand.

The man had a harsh, lined face with deep-set, almost hollow eyes. Canyon moved almost alongside him, but saw no recognition in the quick, hard glance the man threw him.

"I smell smoke on you, mister," Canyon said quietly, "the kind that comes from setting stables on fire. You've got some answering to do, cousin."

The man's eyes fastened on him and comprehension leapt through his face along with a flash of fear. Canyon hadn't expected the blow, or the speed of it, as the man whirled and threw a looping right. Canyon ducked, but the punch grazed his temple. He spun away and glimpsed the others at the bar diving for safety as the man tried to follow with a vicious left hook. Canyon pulled back from the blow and brought up his own, short uppercut. It didn't land squarely, the man was too close, and Canyon had to weave away from a left and right the man threw at him. But the man was charging now, Canyon saw, emboldened with a kind of desperate confidence.

Canyon gave ground, avoided a hard left hook, weaved away from another, and then brought up a tremendous hook from a low angle. It smashed into the man's jaw and he staggered, hands dropping low. Canyon's short right followed through at the same place. The man fell onto his hands and knees, stayed there for a moment, his head shaking, and then he dropped facedown on the floor.

He lay there, motionless, and Canyon turned to the bartender, who looked on with his eyes wide. "Water, please," Canyon said to the barkeep, who filled a white porcelain pitcher. Canyon stepped toward the bar to take it from him. He was reaching for the pitcher when his acute hearing caught the sound, a soft scrape, a heel against the wood floor, and then metal rubbing against leather. Canyon whirled, saw that the figure on the floor had turned over and the six-gun in the man's hand had already cleared the holster.

Canyon O'Grady's draw had the speed and fluidity of a leaping flame, and the ivory-gripped Colt seemed to fire while still in motion. The shot caught the man full in the chest and sent him sliding back across the floor, still half-sitting up while his own shot went wildly into the air. His chest was a gaping red hole, and he came up against the foot of the bar and lay still, the gun still in his lifeless hand.

The bartender's voice broke the silence. "He

won't be answering any questions now, mister,'' the man said.

"It would seem not,'' Canyon agreed, and holstered the big Colt.

"Jesus,'' the barkeep breathed as he leaned over to look at the sprawled figure, and then he barked orders to one of his assistants. "Get him out of here and call Jeb to haul him away,'' he said. He turned back to Canyon as the saloon began to return to normal, the interruption apparently all too ordinary. "That was some shooting, mister. You got a name?'' the man asked.

"Canyon O'Grady,'' the big man said. "You know who he was?''

"Nope, never saw him before. But a lot of strangers pass this way. Missouri's always been the gateway to the West,'' the barkeep said. "It's worse, now. The state's a tinderbox. That's why we need to elect a strong senator from this district.''

"Such as?'' Canyon asked.

"Roy Gannet, of course,'' the barkeep said. "I know, some of his ways bother people. He's a little heavy-handed, but we need a strong man who's not afraid to get his way.''

"Guess you'll find out if everyone feels that way when election time comes.'' Canyon smiled. "Meanwhile, I'll have a whiskey.''

"Coming up,'' the bartender said. "That was the fastest draw I ever saw, mister.''

Canyon smiled at the unsaid. "I'm no gunhand, if that's what you're wondering. But being fast comes in handy if you like living, and I do,'' the big red-haired man said as he took his drink to a small table in the corner. He sat down, nursed the whiskey, then had a second and let it last him through the remainder of the evening. But the only visitors he had were two of the floor girls, who finally decided he was no prospect and drifted away.

Canyon rose when the night slid into the early-morning hours. "Time to go," he murmured to himself. "There'll be no meeting tonight." He strolled from the saloon with a nod to the bartender, who, he decided, probably owned the place. Outside, he swung onto the palomino and rode from the town. He found a rocky, wall-like formation covered with burned ground moss and settled down behind it where a stand of dogwood offered quiet shelter. He was asleep on his bedroll in minutes, the night breeze Mother Nature's lullaby.

Morning's warm sun woke him and he found a stream, washed in the invigorating water, and let the sun help dry him. A stand of black grapes afforded a fresh and sweet breakfast, and finally he moved out across the Missouri countryside. He swung onto a road that led to the ranch house, and when he reached it, he saw three men at work replacing the doors on the stables and the barn.

The white-haired man, a bandage across the front of his head that almost matched his hair, waved at Canyon as the palomino came to a halt. "Never did get to thank you proper last night," he said, hurrying forward. "Tad Elkins is the name."

"Glad I was close enough to help," Canyon

said, and lifted his glance to the young woman, who came from the house. Her face was even prettier than he had remembered, and still as pugnacious. The tomboy was still in the swagger of her walk, he saw, but a very feminine shape was covered by a red-checked shirt and tight Levi's that clung to a firm figure. She halted before him as he swung to the ground, her level, steady eyes grave.

"Glenda Taylor," she said, and extended her hand in a warm, firm grip.

"Canyon O'Grady," he said.

She studied him for a moment, steady brown eyes roaming across the length and breadth of him. "It's a name that fits you, big man. And a name to make one ask questions about you."

"Ask." Canyon smiled.

"Later, perhaps," Glenda Taylor said.

"Meanwhile I'll do my own asking. You run this spread by yourself, Glenda?" Canyon questioned.

"I do," she answered.

"Why were those night-riders trying to set your place on fire?" Canyon asked.

"I can only guess at that, Canyon O'Grady. Please come inside with me," Glenda said, and he followed her into the ranch house, where he found a modestly furnished room, leather couch and leather chairs, heavy walnut sideboard. The frilled curtains were the only feminine touch.

"Make a guess," Canyon pressed, and Glenda Taylor faced him, high, compact breasts pushing the red-checkered shirt out as she drew in a deep sigh.

"A number of ranchers around here are very unhappy with me," she said. "Ben Stodger most of all. But my own father's very unhappy with me."

Canyon felt the furrow cross his brow. "Surely you don't think your own father did that?" he asked with astonishment in his voice.

Glenda shrugged, a grimness in her face. "I wouldn't put it past him," she said. "I was away. I wouldn't have been hurt."

"Strong words."

"Strong feelings."

"Why is everyone so unhappy with you?" Canyon asked.

"Come, I'll show you," she said, turned on her heel, and led the way through a corridor of the house to a side door that opened onto one of the stables. He followed at her heels and quickly noted that all the stalls were double-width. She halted at the first stall and he saw the two horses, reddish chestnut in color with light manes; stocky of build and close coupled, they exuded both power and energy. One a stallion, the other a mare, he noted, and both were quick to respond to the young woman's presence. But they were unlike any horse he had ever seen, slightly dish-faced, yet with no signs of Arab in them.

"Haflingers," Glenda said crisply. "An Austrian breed, originally developed in the mountains of the Tyrol. These horses are strong and tough, yet nimble enough to move through the hardest mountain terrain, and yet eat half of what an ordinary horse eats."

She moved on to the next stall, which held a

considerably larger horse, deep-chested with good quarters and a refined head. Small ears and powerful legs were part of a reddish-brown animal of power and latent grace. "A Cleveland bay from England," Glenda said. "This is a fine horse for cross-breeding. Cleveland bays are natural jumpers and they outlive most other breeds." She moved on to the next double stall and the smile came to the big flame-haired man's lips at once as he gazed at the two charcoal-black mounts with their wide faces, long, wavy-curled manes, intelligent, dark eyes, and powerful, chunky bodies.

"Connemara ponies," Canyon said, and Glenda Taylor nodded. "I know the breed well. A friend of my father's raised them in Ireland."

"They're really too big to be called ponies in my estimation," Glenda said. "Of all the breeds, they're probably the hardiest. They live outdoors all year 'round in northwest Ireland and thrive on the meager grasses and salt-marsh weeds. Their feet are so hard they seldom need shoeing and they're as surefooted as a mountain goat."

"So they are," Canyon said. "And these are two fine specimens." He moved closer, stroked the horses, and ran his hands over their firm, strong coats. "I suppose you know the popular fancy that they cross-bred with the horses that came from the ships of the Spanish Armada that were wrecked off the Irish coast."

"That's what I've always heard," Glenda said.

"Not so," Canyon said. "Those horses that made shore were all Andalusian, which would mean they were descended from the Arab stock.

Looking at a Connemara pony will tell you it has no Arab blood in it. It descended from the horses of Northern Europe and the wild horses of Mongolia. There are records kept by the old Christian brothers that prove it.''

"You know your horses, Canyon O'Grady, but then I was sure of that from that palomino you ride," Glenda said, and beckoned him to the last wide stall. "My pride of them all," she said, and Canyon's eyes roved over a tall horse, blackish-bay in color, with long and elegant lines, yet with power in the forequarters and rump. The horse watched its visitors with calmness and confidence that was almost disdain. "This is a Kabardine from the Caucasus Mountains of Russia," Glenda said. "I've two mares out in the corrals. These are among the breeds the Cossacks rode. Until they're brought in for breaking to the saddle, Kabardines live wild in the mountains. They are known to have greater endurance than any other Russian breed, and the Russians breed for endurance.'' She led the way outside where he saw more of the unusual breeds in the corrals along with a handful of Morgans and quarter horses. "My breeding program includes some cross-breeding with domestic stock," Glenda explained.

"You're telling me that the horse ranchers around here don't want you breeding these animals you've brought in," Canyon said.

"That's right," the young woman snapped. "They're afraid. All they do is keep breeding their Morgans and quarter horses. They're thinning out the stock, ruining endurance, agility, stamina, intelligence. They're keeping too restricted a breeding pool, for one thing, and they're breeding horses that don't have enough of the qualities needed to begin with."

"You think you could change all that," Canyon said, and saw determination flare in her eyes.

"I know I could. I've spent a lot of money and time bringing this foundation stock here. Cross-bred carefully and properly with our own wild horses, they could produce better animals in almost every way," Glenda said. "But Ben Stodger and most of the others don't care about that. They'd rather just keep selling inferior stock. That's why they're afraid of me. They see me as a threat, and they want to put me out of business."

"And that includes your own father, you say?" Canyon asked. "He's one of those ranchers?"

"He has connections to them, and he has his own reasons for wanting me to quit," Glenda said, and the hardness of her face told Canyon she'd not be elaborating further. She gestured for him to follow her back into the house.

"Seems like this is a pretty big job for one person to be running alone, especially somebody surrounded by enemies," he said.

"I've Tad," Glenda said, then paused at the chiding glance Canyon tossed her. "All right, he's not exactly protection, but he's an old friend and he's all I can afford. Buying the stock has cost me a lot. My mother left me a yearly inheritance when she died. I've spent the next two years of it on my horses." She paused again, turned, and came close to him. "I've enough left to hire you, Canyon O'Grady. One of the workmen told me what happened at the saloon last night. News travels fast around here.''

"So it seems,'' Canyon said. "Nobody knew him, least they didn't admit to it.''

"I never saw the others you shot here, either. They were hired outsiders, I'd guess,'' Glenda said. "Will you come work for me? I'll find the money to pay you well.''

"Sorry.'' Canyon smiled apologetically and drew a quick frown.

"You've another job around here?'' she asked.

"Not around here in particular,'' Canyon said.

"Somewhere else, then?''

"Not anywhere else in particular, either.''

"You're not making much sense,'' Glenda snapped.

"My work is everywhere. I'm a wanderer, a man of odd jobs, a mender of whatever needs mending,'' he said.

"You go around finding good deeds to do?'' Glenda said, her eyes narrowed at him. "Such as last night?''

"Exactly, lass. It's how I take my pleasure,'' Canyon said.

A faint touch of amusement came into her eyes and he was suddenly reminded of how Carla Gannet had studied him. "A most unusual philosophy,'' she commented.

"I'm far from the first to have it. The English poet John Wesley put it in a fine way. 'Do all the good you can,' he said. 'By all the means you can, in all the ways you can, in all the places you can, at all the times you can, to all the people you can, as long as ever you can.' "

"A wanderer who can quote the poets and rides a horse fit for a king. Why doesn't that hang together?" she slid at him.

He shrugged. "Things fit, in their own ways," Canyon said. "But I'll help you all I can while I'm in these parts."

"You can't always be in the right place at the right time, Canyon O'Grady," Glenda said.

"I'll do my best," he said. "I might pay a visit to some of the ranchers who're so unhappy with you. Maybe I'll learn something."

"But on your own," Glenda said. "You won't go to work for me, let me pay you."

"That's right." Canyon smiled, and suddenly her arms were around his neck. Her lips pressed softly against his, the kiss restrained yet holding promise, and he felt the softness of her high, firm breasts against his chest. She pulled away in a moment, a faint smile on her lips.

"That's a thank-you for last night," she said. "Not just for what you did, but for what you are."

"And what's that?" He chuckled.

"A liar. A handsome rogue. A fascinating question mark." Glenda laughed.

"As good a description as a man can hope for," Canyon O'Grady said with a bow. "I'll be stopping back."

"Good. I'd like that," Glenda Taylor replied, and walked to the palomino with him. "I'd like to know more about you."

"We'll learn more about each other," he said,

then swung onto the horse and slowly rode from the ranch, his gaze scanning the two Kabardine mares in one of the corrals.

This land held surprises at every turn, he decided as he sent the palomino across a low slope and down to the road. Its people were as complex as its politics. It was a place of crosscurrents, some clear to the eye, others swirling in hidden depths. Glenda Taylor was one of the latter, and he'd be stopping back for another visit, he was certain.

He saw the three horsemen appear from a ridge low and to the left. They were coming toward him, and he continued on at the same slow trot. But when they reached the road in front of him, his hand rested on the butt of the ivory-gripped Colt. He halted as the riders reined up in front of him.

"Been looking for you, mister. Our boss would like to see you," the one said.

"Who might that be?" Canyon asked calmly.

"Hal Colbert," the man said, and it was an effort for Canyon to keep the surprise from his face.

"You know what he wants with me?" he asked.

"Nope," the man said, and Canyon shrugged.

"Then let's find out. I'll follow," he said, and fell in close behind the three horsemen.

They led the way over another hillside, down to a wide road lined with box elder, and finally turned into a broad entranceway where a modest ranch house waited. There was a stable to one side, and a hitching post where a dozen horses were tethered. As they reined to a halt, a tall man with a narrow body came from the house. He wore black trousers, a white shirt, and black suspenders, his face was long and thin, with a narrow nose, pale-blue eyes, and carefully combed, thick black hair. It was a professorial face, but Canyon felt there was steel under its mild appearance.

"You fit the description, Canyon O'Grady," the man said. "I'm Hal Colbert." Canyon nodded and made no move to leave the saddle. "I heard about the incident at the Dry Corn Kitten last night. One of my men happened to be there," Colbert said. "It was apparently quite impressive."

"It was what had to be done," Canyon said.

Hal Colbert's smile was carefully controlled. "The very good can afford to be modest," he said. "These are strenuous times and I am involved in many things. I could use a man with your talents working for me."

"Doing what?" Canyon asked.

"Whatever needs doing," Colbert replied. "You are apparently a man who is quick, resourceful and not easily impressed. I'll pay top dollar."

"I'd like to know more about what you might use me for. I don't sign on as a gunhand," Canyon said to draw the man out further.

"I can't say what you'd be called on to do. There are too many possibilities," Hal Colbert answered, and Canyon smiled inwardly. The man wasn't about to limit himself with the wrong answer.

"I'll think about it, Mr. Colbert," Canyon said. "That's the best I can do now."

"Well, that's better than a refusal." Colbert smiled. "I'd just ask you not to take a job with anyone else before giving me another chance."

"Fair enough," Canyon said, then nodded and turned the palomino away, put the horse into a trot, and rode down the broad entranceway and onto the road. Only when he was far enough away did he allow himself a broad smile. It was astonishing how the players were lining up for him, he reflected. Avenues were opening up in every direction. But Carla Gannet was the first to be explored, he reminded himself, not that he needed a reminder as the long, raven's-wing hair and alabaster skin swam through his mind.

He kept the palomino straight on the road into town and slowed only when he reached the crowded street of Dry Corn. He found the general store, dismounted, and hurried inside, where the storekeeper nodded at his request.

"A fancy shirt? Yep, we have a few," the man said.

"Not too fancy," Canyon corrected quickly, and the man slid two ruffled shirts back onto a shelf and pulled out a silk one with a full collar, billowy sleeves, and a flowing black cravat. "That'll do. Maybe I'll get to wear it again someplace else," Canyon said. "I hate buying a shirt for just one occasion and I sure won't be wearing this on the range."

"I'd guess you were going to one of the parties tonight," the storekeeper said as he wrapped the shirt.

"One of the parties?" Canyon frowned.

"Lots of folks are holding affairs tonight. Tomorrow's festival day and the annual race meet," the man said, and handed Canyon the shirt. "Big doings this time every year."

"Obliged." Canyon nodded and hurried outside, the shirt tucked under one arm. He was beginning to look forward to the evening. But, then, who wouldn't look forward to another meeting with the beautiful Carla Gannet. If only it could stay as simple as that, he sighed as he rode from town.

4

The big, red-haired figure rode slowly through the early-night darkness, the silk of the fancy shirt soft against his body. He was about to plunge into the very center of things, Canyon O'Grady realized, much more quickly than he'd expected, thanks to a runaway horse. As he rode, he let his thoughts wind backward, to the moment that had brought him here.

No meeting in the Oval Office this time, with its rich furniture of American craftsmen that President Buchanan had brought in to replace the French-made pieces. The message had reached him and brought him to the street corner just outside the Capitol. There he found the black Twelve-Quarter coach, a four-horse team in the shafts, black curtains drawn on the gracefully shaped windows.

The uniformed soldiers admitted him into the long coach, where he eased into the cushioned seat across from the white-haired man, whose unruly tuft of hair and bright-blue eyes marked him at once.

"Mister President," Canyon said, and James Buchanan leaned back against the thickly upholstered seat of the coach. Another man sat beside him, a thin-faced man with rimless eyeglasses who exuded both quiet competence and stuffiness.

"You know my aide, Bill Tardun," President Buchanan said.

"I do that." Canyon nodded, and Tardun allowed a stiff smile.

President James Buchanan leaned forward, his head slightly held to one side in the manner characteristic of him. "How are you at walking on eggs, Agent O'Grady?" he asked.

"I've done it," Canyon answered. "Broken a few, too," he admitted.

"You'll probably break a few on this assignment," the president said. "We've a delicate situation to deal with in the state of Missouri."

"I've been there," Canyon said.

"Then you know the state is half-slave and half-free, a seedbed of conflicting interests. With all the talk about secession down there, we're very concerned that Missouri maintains its balance. We certainly don't want its legislature loaded with slave-state advocates."

"I'd guess not," Canyon agreed.

"There's an all-important election for senator coming up in the northern part of the state," Bill Tardun put in. "One of the men running is a wealthy rancher, Roy Gannet. He's a powerful force in the district, but word has reached us that, under the surface, he was strong ties with the slave part of the state. If this is so and he's elected, we're in trouble."

"Who's running against him?" Canyon asked.

"Hal Colbert, a small rancher, teaches Sunday school. Our information has it that Colbert is strictly a free-state advocate. Naturally, he's the man we want to see elected," President Buchanan said.

Canyon felt the furrow travel across his brow. "You want me to go down there and see to that?"

"Good Lord, no," the president protested. "This is the delicate part. We can't openly help either man, but we're told that Gannet is using terror and violence to win. You're being sent to put a stop to that."

"In other words, to keep the election honest."

"More accurately, to give Hal Colbert the chance to make an honest win," President Buchanan said. "All without officially taking sides."

"I understand now what you meant about walking on eggs," Canyon murmured.

"If you find out that Roy Gannet's trying to steal the election, put an end to it and give Colbert a chance," the president said. "There will be three polling places set up in the district. The election machinery isn't geared for more than that. The most important will be in a town called Dry Corn. That's where most of the people in the district will vote. It's central to all the surrounding towns and outlying homes. It's also right in the heart of Roy Gannet's territory."

"We have an informant there," Bill Tardun cut in. "He'll make contact with you at the saloon in Dry Corn by night. He'll fill you in on what's going on."

Canyon nodded and the rest of the conversation had been concerned with the mechanics of meeting the informant. Finally Canyon had stepped from the long-bodied, graceful coach. He watched the coach roll away, the windows remaining curtained.

Canyon's thoughts snapped off as he halted on a low hillock. He'd gone through Dry Corn and asked directions to the Gannet place, but it hardly proved necessary. A large, diffused glow of light appeared ahead of him, spreading horizontally like a low cloud. It took shape as he rode closer, and it became strings of lawn lights, some brightly colored lanterns, each with its own candle. Behind the lights, he saw the brightly lighted house, imposing with two pillars in the front and a wing jutting out from each side. It was a mansion of a house. He heard the sound of a guitar and fiddle band drift toward him, and he spurred the palomino forward until he reached the lighted lawn area. To one side, he noted the rows of carriages, a few buckboards, but most of them Essex traps, canopy-topped phaetons, and at least a half-dozen Stanhopes.

He tethered the palomino among the wagons and strolled across the lawn, past men and women in fancy clothes, the men in dress suits, all of the women in long gowns. He had reached the pillars of the house when the tall, slender figure appeared in the entranceway and came toward him. Her long black hair was pulled back and held in place by two pearl clips, a form-fitting black dress heightening the alabaster whiteness of her skin. She wiped the surprise from her eyes with a smile.

"You've come. I wasn't sure you would," she said.

"I said I would," he answered, and her smile widened.

"A touch of reproof. I accept," Carla Gannet said, and her eyes moved across him again. "A fancy shirt and all. I'm impressed."

"A concession to formality," Canyon said, "and nothing compared to what I see here," he added as his gaze swept the richly gowned women and the men in fancy-dress outfits.

Carla linked her arm in his and steered him into a big room where furniture had been cleared away to turn it into a ballroom. His gaze swept the paintings on the walls, each in its own gold-leafed frame, big canvases of landscapes and formal portraits. The tall windows were framed with dark-red drapes of heavy velvet. It was an opulent room filled with opulent guests, but he took time to enjoy the way Carla Gannet's very white breasts rose up from the neckline of the gown in lovely twin mounds.

"Daddy," she called out and a man turned to her, resplendent in a wine-colored frock coat and frilled shirt. Canyon found himself facing a big man, broad-chested with a wide face that edged jowliness. His eyes, dark brown, were sharp and quick. "This is Canyon O'Grady, the man I told you about," Carla introduced.

"Glad to meet you, O'Grady. I've been waiting to thank you for saving Carla from that rotten-tempered horse," the man said in a booming, sonorous voice. His handshake was strong and he radiated an air of booming heartiness.

"Canyon says the horse has been mishandled. That didn't make Owen happy when I told him," Carla said.

"I know, and you didn't have to tell him, Carla," Roy Gannet said. "You like sticking pins in people."

"Only when they deserve it. Owen acted horribly," the young woman said.

Canyon saw Roy Gannet take him in with a glance that missed nothing, despite its quickness. "This isn't a night for talk, but why don't you come visit again if you're staying in these parts, Canyon O'Grady?" the man boomed.

"I will be around for a spell," Canyon said. "And I'll come by."

"Good," Roy Gannet said. "You a ranching man, O'Grady?"

"Not really."

"A wrangler, perhaps?"

"Can't really say that, either."

"You ride trail?"

"Not really." Canyon smiled and saw the questioning frown form on Roy Gannet's brow.

"Canyon is a wanderer, Father," Carla said with sweet sarcasm. "Whatever that means."

Roy Gannet shook off the answer. "I'm running for senator and I can always use help. I'm sure I can find something to fit your talents, O'Grady. You just come visit," he said, then turned away and shouted another booming greeting to a nearby man and woman. His warmth seemed natural enough, but Roy Gannet was the kind of man who could manufacture heartiness, Canyon was certain.

Carla steered him to two long tables that served as a bar. She dipped a glass into the punch bowl while he took a whiskey from an elderly black man in a butler's outfit.

"You could do worse than work for Daddy. He pays top dollar, gives fine board, and treats his men well," Carla said.

"But that'd make it difficult for you." Canyon smiled.

"What do you mean?" she asked as they strolled from the bar.

"Appearances are important to you. To your pa, too. How will you go out riding with the help?" Canyon asked.

Carla Gannet's thin eyebrows lifted in a lovely arch as she gave him a quietly amused glance. "And you think I'd like to do that with you?"

"I do." He smiled.

"Conceit large enough to match your charm, I'd say," she remarked.

"No conceit at all."

"What would you call it?"

"Paying attention to the eyes instead of the lips." He laughed. "Seeing. Sensing. Knowing."

"Then denial is pointless," she returned.

"Exactly. When do we go riding?"

Her answer was interrupted by a voice, harsh and angry, and Canyon turned to see Owen Dunstan, his tall form in a black dinner suit, his handsome face tight with disdainful superiority.

"You've your nerve coming here," Dunstan barked.

"He is here at my invitation," Carla Gannet said firmly, and Canyon saw Owen Dunstan turn to her with sneering reproof.

"Is he to be another of your indulgences, Carla?" Dunstan said.

"He's a guest here," Carla Gannet said, and Canyon saw Roy Gannet's sharp eyes narrow as his attention turned to Dunstan.

Owen Dunstan turned to the big, red-haired man with a sneer of pained tolerance. "Carla always wants to make a silk purse out of a sow's ear. I have to keep showing her that's not possible."

Dunstan's inference was hardly subtle. Canyon smiled inwardly, and his muscles tightened as he longed to smash the words back into the man's supercilious face. But that would be only playing into his hands, and the stakes were too important for that.

"How do you show her that? Words are cheap," Canyon said.

"I'll have to show her the difference again," Dunstan said.

"The difference between what?" Canyon pressed.

"Quality and a piece of luck, the skill of real riding against an exhibition of crude wrangling, but mostly, the superiority of good breeding over peasant stock. I'll give you a gentleman's challenge. Ride against me in the meet tomorrow," Dunstan said.

"The meet?" Canyon frowned, and it was Carla who answered.

"Owen's talking about the Missouri Challenge Cup meet," she said. "The race has been an annual fixture for twenty years. Anyone can enter, but it's unfair of Owen to challenge you," Carla said. "Only the finest mounts enter, top-quality riders, and it's a terribly brutal course, full of dangerous jumps."

Canyon's eyes went to Owen Dunstan's faint sneer. "You riding that mount of yours, the one I saw yesterday?"

"That's right," Dunstan said.

Canyon smiled. "Sounds tempting," he murmured, and it was Roy Gannet's voice that cut in.

"Don't be talked into something you'll regret, O'Grady," the man said. "You did fine things for Carla yesterday. Let it stay there. Owen's my associate, but he can be right cruel. He's won the last five meets and Ben Stodger has come second or third the last five times. The best horses in northern Missouri will be there."

"Only if I enter," Canyon said, and was rewarded with Roy Gannet's booming laugh.

"The man has wit to go with his spirit," Roy roared.

"What do I have to do to enter?" Canyon asked.

"Just show up," Roy Gannet said.

"I'll think about it," Canyon said, and watched the triumphant smile spread across Owen Dunstan's face.

"I see you do know your place, O'Grady,"

the man said. "That shows a certain amount of crude intelligence."

"And you've shown nothing but a fishwife's tongue and the disposition of a nervous whore," Canyon said, and watched Owen Dunstan's face grow red.

"Gentlemen, that's enough. You're both my guests," Roy Gannet cut in and Dunstan spun on his heel and strode away.

"Walk with me, Canyon," Carla said, and took his arm as she strolled away. "Owen's noticed the way you look at me. He gets very nervous when a handsome man takes an interest in me."

Canyon smiled. Carla Gannet was the kind who liked a challenge. It was in the contained amusement with which she viewed the world, in the sensuousness she exuded yet kept under control.

"Is he nervous about himself or about you?" he slid out, and she smiled.

"Maybe some of both," she answered.

"This Missouri Challenge meet, what do I get if I win?" he asked.

"The silver cup, of course, and the winner's ribbons," Carla said.

Canyon half-shrugged. "I don't race for cups or ribbons. We common folk want a prize we can enjoy," he said.

"Such as?" she questioned, pinpoints of light in her black eyes.

"The comfort of a bag of gold, the pleasure of a keg of good whiskey, or the arms of a warm woman," Canyon said. "Now that makes a race worth winning."

Her black eyes stayed on him and a faint smile edged her lips. "That's a charming way of backing out of something, I'll say that much," she observed.

"I'm not backing anywhere. I can win," Canyon said.

"Nonsense," Carla snapped. "You haven't a chance."

"Make the winning worthwhile and I'll show you," he said evenly. "Put the rest of you where your mouth is."

The pinpoints of light flared in the black orbs as she met his gaze. "You think I'd be afraid?" she questioned. "You're wrong."

"Show me," he said. "I win, you're mine for a night."

"And if you lose?" Carla asked.

"You'll have another kind of satisfaction, and prove Owen Dunstan's point for him." Canyon smiled as Carla Gannet's eyes narrowed at him.

"Yes, it would be a kind of satisfaction to make you eat some of that conceited charm, but frankly, that's not enough," she said. "You see, Canyon O'Grady, I don't buy any of that happy wanderer or tinker story, not from the likes of you. You suddenly turn up here out of nowhere. There has to be a reason. There's a lot going on around here. Maybe you're one of Hal Colbert's new men. I don't know, and I'm sure you won't be telling me, so I'll put it this way: you win and you win me; you lose and you leave here after the race and don't come back."

Canyon let his lips purse in thought. She had put another dimension on it, a much more dangerous one, not that she was aware of that. He knew Washington wouldn't appreciate his endangering his mission on a wager, and there was only one way to win a horserace and a hundred ways to lose one. Yet Carla Gannet could be his way inside Roy Gannet's operation. Nothing ventured, nothing gained, lad, he murmured inwardly, and turned a wide smile on Carla. "You won't enjoy losing," he said. "But you'll enjoy paying up."

Her eyes held his, her lovely face growing serious for a moment, and he saw her take a deep breath, the alabaster breasts rising high under the neckline of the dress and tiny dots of color touching her cheeks. "It seems we have a wager," she said.

"We do, a wager worth making for a prize worth winning." Canyon grinned happily.

"Compliments won't count tomorrow," she said.

"Compliments always count," Canyon said. "They linger, when everything else leaves."

She laughed, the low, rich sound again. "I'll leave on that. I have to play hostess," she said. "I'll see you later. Enjoy yourself."

"I'll not be staying long," he said, and watched her glide away, narrow-hipped rear encased in the black gown. She walked more sensuously than most women danced as she wandered through the crowded room filled with finely gowned and attractive women.

Owen Dunstan sent a disdainful glance Canyon's way while talking to an older man, and O'Grady smiled as he made his way to the open door and out onto the lighted lawn. He saw Roy Gannet nearby, heard his booming, hearty laughter as he conversed with a trio of friends.

Canyon had just started across the lawn when the figure stepped into his path, a light-beige dress with puffed sleeves and a full skirt with ruffles across the high, round breastline of it. His lips parted in surprise that was echoed in the medium-brown eyes that frowned at him. "Glenda Taylor," he breathed. "Didn't expect to see you here."

"I'm always invited, but I certainly didn't expect to see you here," Glenda said.

"Carla Gannet invited me," he told her, and a tiny frown crossed her brow as she stared back.

"The surprise of the evening for me," she said with a trace of asperity in her voice.

"I saved her neck from a very angry horse yesterday," Canyon said.

"I see," Glenda said guardedly when Roy Gannet's hearty voice broke in and Canyon saw the man approaching, his wide face wreathed in a grin but his eyes sharp.

"You do get around for a man new in these parts, Mr. O'Grady," Gannet said. "You know my other daughter, too."

Canyon knew his quick glance at Glenda was filled with astonishment, but she seemed utterly unperturbed as she looked at Roy Gannet. "Good evening, Father," she said quietly.

"I didn't know whether you'd come," Gannet said to her.

"I've never missed one of these. Why would I start now?" she asked with a sweetness laced with icy politeness. "It's one of the few times I get to see some of my supposed friends."

"Now, Glenda, let's not start that," Gannet said, some of the heartiness deserting him.

"Just stating facts, Father," Glenda said, and Roy Gannet turned to Canyon, then back to Glenda.

"How'd you come to know this handsome newcomer?" he asked.

"A chance meeting," Glenda said quickly and firmly. Canyon nodded agreement.

Roy Gannet turned to him. "Will you come watch the race tomorrow?" he asked. "It's a festive time."

"I'll do more than watch." Canyon smiled, and Roy Gannet frowned.

"You surprise me, O'Grady. I took you for a man who knew when to back away. In fact, I thought you had," he said.

"Never put it in words," Canyon said.

"No, you didn't," Roy Gannet conceded with a wry smile. "See you tomorrow, then."

He strode back to his guests and Canyon turned to Glenda immediately, a frown on his brow. "I'd say you've some explaining to do, lass."

"Not here," she said.

"Want to tell me why you said you were Glenda Taylor?"

"Come visit me," she said almost crossly.

"Count on it," Canyon growled and watched her walk away, halt, and talk to two young women.

He made his way to the palomino, the surprise still clinging to him as he rode from the noise and the music. He certainly would be visiting Glenda again, but it would have to wait. He wanted the horse to have a good night in a comfortable stable before the race. He reached town, halted at the stable, where a sleepy-eyed man took the horse into a comfortable stall. "Feed him now. Nothing in the morning," Canyon instructed.

"Yes, sir," the man said, and Canyon hurried away to the narrow frame building that advertised bed and board on its shingle. He took a room on the ground floor, found a neat bed and a dresser with a porcelain pitcher of water atop it. He shed his clothes and stretched out on the bed, turned off the small lamp, and let himself relax in the darkness.

He had almost fallen asleep when the knock came at the door, soft but firm, and he swung long legs from the bed with a frown. He stepped into trousers, and the ivory-gripped Colt was in his hand when he opened the door. The frown dug deeper into his forehead when he saw the figure in the light-beige dress with the puffed sleeves. Glenda's pert face was grave as she peered up at him.

"May I come in?" she asked, and he pulled the door wider.

"How'd you know I was here?" he growled, and closed the door as she stepped into the small room. He turned the lamp up and saw her eyes take in the breadth of his shoulders and the contours of his muscled chest.

"I didn't. I took a chance. I stopped at the stable and asked if a man had brought in a fine palomino tonight," she said, and her eyes continued to enjoy the naked symmetry of his torso.

"Why'd you come? I told you I'd be visiting," Canyon said.

"But not before the meet. I came to tell you not to enter," Glenda said.

"The line forms at the right."

"They have their reasons. I'm thinking about you."

"That's nice. Any special reason for that?"

"You did me a big favor. I'd like to repay it. You'll only make a fool of yourself if you race. You'll give Owen Dunstan a chance to laugh at you," Glenda said.

"Maybe," Canyon said as he put the Colt back into the holster hanging from the bedpost.

"What made you decide to enter?" Glenda asked, peering at him from under lowered brows.

"A whim. A moment of rashness."

"My foot," Glenda snapped. "Carla talked you into it, didn't she?"

"I wouldn't put it exactly that way." Canyon smiled.

"Put it any way you like, but that's what happened. Don't you see, she's only trying to make a fool out of you. She likes to do things like that."

"Why?"

"It makes her feel superior. She and Owen Dunstan are the same, peas in a pod."

"I get the feeling you don't care for your sister," Canyon commented, and sat down on the bed.

Instant anger flooded Glenda's eyes, and she sat down beside him with a flounce that made her high breasts bounce. "Carla, the favorite one? Carla, the beautiful one? No, I don't like her much. Things grew worse after Ma died. She became a greater favorite of Father's. She enjoys the same things he does: power, wealth, fancy parties, fancy clothes. That's one reason I left and went out on my own."

"And called yourself Glenda Taylor?"

"That's my name, my married name," she said, and Canyon felt the surprise flash in his face.

"You've a husband?" He frowned.

"Had a husband. For one day," Glenda said bitterly.

"What happened?"

"He was killed."

"How?"

"An accident, they called it," she said.

Canyon peered at her darkened face, her lips drawn tight against each other. "You think otherwise?"

"Yes. I did then and I do now," she flung back angrily.

"Want to tell me about it?" he asked gently.

"When you come visiting," she said, closing off the subject. "I just stopped by to tell you not to race, but it seems I've wasted my time."

He reached out and cupped her chin with one hand. "Thanks for trying," he said.

Glenda's medium-brown eyes peered hard at him. "Why are you doing this, Canyon O'Grady? Who are you? You've a reason," she said.

"I like surprising people and I like to win," he answered glibly.

"Not good enough. You've more in mind."

He ignored her persistence and rose with her as she started toward the door, where she turned to face him. Her hands came to press against the smooth muscles of his chest. "I'd have you stay if it weren't for the race. I'll be needing some sleep," he said.

"What makes you think I would?" she returned as her palms stayed against his chest.

"Would you?"

"You're going to sleep, so I've no need to answer that," she said crisply.

"Saved by a horserace." Canyon laughed.

She reached up, her arms suddenly lifting to encircle his neck, and her lips found his, lingered with a soft pressure, and then she pulled back. "That's for luck for tomorrow," Glenda said, and hurried from the room before he had a chance to answer. She went down the hall, not looking back.

He closed the door, shed his trousers and stretched out on the bed. She was concerned for him, he was convinced, but the visit had been more than that. She believed Carla had set him up to enjoy his fall, and she was really trying to deny Carla another victory. He was the newest pawn in a bitter rivalry. But it was a game he could perhaps use to his own advantage, he mused, and snapped off thoughts to turn on his side and draw sleep around himself. The new day would take all his skills and wisdom.

He slept well and woke with the dawn sun, washed, dressed, and hurried to the stable. He took a hoof pick from his saddlebag and went over the horse's feet until he'd cleaned away every bit of trail crud still clinging to the hooves. With the stableman watching, he uncorked a stoppered vial from his saddlebag, poured a little of the contents into his hands and began to massage the horse's legs, starting just below the brisket and going down to the fetlock. "Pennyroyal, comfrey root, chamomile, strawberry leaf, and white willow bark," Canyon said. "It invigorates every muscle within a few hours."

"You must be entering the race," the stableman said.

"I am." Canyon nodded as he finally finished with the last hind leg, closed the bottle, and returned it to his saddlebag. "Works for people, too," he said as he saddled the horse, adjusted the cinch, and climbed into the saddle.

"Go straight south, turn left at the pond, and you'll see the flags and poles a hundred yards on," the stableman said. "But you'll be early."

"I know." Canyon smiled and moved the palomino slowly down the road.

The workmen were still setting up the long wood benches that would be the spectator seats, while others were festooning the grandstand with ribbons and stringing up the finish line. A man in a black bowler hat sat at the square table with the ledger book and the sign that read EN-TRIES. He heard a firm, clear voice singing and he looked up, peered down the road, and saw the lone rider on the bronzed horse that gleamed in the morning sun. The man's song came clearer as he neared.

It's there you'll see the pipers and
  the fiddlers competin',
the nimble-footed dancers and their
  trippin' on the daisies,
And others crying cigars and lights
  and bills for all the races,
  and the colors of the jockeys
  and the price and horse's ages . . .

The man in the bowler hat broke into a wide smile as the big redheaded man drew to a halt in front of his table. " 'The Galaway Races.' It's been a long time since these old ears have heard that,'' he said.

'' 'The Galaway Races' it is indeed,'' the big man atop the palomino said.

''Well, we're not as fancy as that here,'' the man said, and lifted the quill pen with his hand.

''Canyon O'Grady riding Cormac,'' the flame-haired man said.

''That'll be one dollar,'' the man said as he wrote the entry into the ledger. ''You're the first to arrive. You'll have more than an hour's wait.''

"I know. I've things to see to," Canyon said, and the man handed him a cardboard square with a number on it to hang on to his back.

"Number One. Hope it brings you luck, O'Grady," the man said. "You'll be needing it."

"I'll be making my own luck." Canyon smiled as he swung from the saddle and tied the horse to a long hitching post set back from the track. "I'll be back for him," he said as he walked onto the raceway, passed under the starting line, and strode on.

A wide, straight path had been smoothed for the start, and Canyon passed the grandstand and the long spectator benches, measured his steps, and moved onto a gentle incline that leveled to a wide turn. The track remained wide as he came to the first jump, a natural post-and-rail fence, not too high, and he only paused briefly at it before going on.

A dozen yards on he came to two more post-and-rail fences, not too high either, and he smiled as he stepped around the hurdle. They seemed deceptively simple, but they were close enough together to hit the forelegs of any horse that didn't take them exactly right. "Some won't," he muttered, and walked on to halt at the next jump. He saw a hogback with its three parallel bars, the center one highest. A hogback deceived many horses and their riders who didn't allow enough height to their leap to clear the center bar, or who didn't put enough length into their jump. But this hogback had an added danger, he saw. It had been placed at a spot where the ground fell away on the other side.

Any horse would go down when it landed unless pulled up fast. Short-legged horses would have the most trouble, and from what he knew of such meets, it was a certainty that many of the horses entered would be short-legged quarter horses and many of their riders wouldn't see the ground fall away until it was too late. The course had been planned to do in all but the finest mounts and the best riders, he realized. He hurried on. A chicken-coop jump came next, not particularly difficult, then another post-and-rails with a sharp turn at the other side.

The course flattened and became a winding, twisting series of sharp turns, and Canyon walked each with deliberate slowness as he made mental notes. At the end of the turns he came to a brush-covered wall, the brush so thick that the stones beneath it were invisible except at close-range inspection. A rider relaxing to let his horse's legs scrape through the top of the brush would hit the stones and go down. He moved on to a hay-bale jump and strode past it, went on, and slowed when he reached a brush-and-water jump. He edged alongside it and saw that the brush had not been placed against the edge of the water as it usually was, but had been set back a good three feet. A horse had to take the jump lengthened full out or hit the water and go down.

Canyon strode on, his head throbbing. The course had been laid out with cruel skill, and he continued to blueprint each and every jump. The last six were double and triple rail jumps, two very close, too close for tired horses, the next two were spread out; and the last jump was a very high triple pole. The course turned and became the flat finishing stretch. As he walked it, he translated time and distance into the strides of the palomino. He drew near to the finish line and saw that the grandstands had become filled, the air buzzing with excitement, and he realized he had been at least an hour on his slow and careful survey. But each jump was imprinted in his mind, each twist and turn of the course committed to memory.

He returned to the palomino, untethered the horse, and made his way past the dozens of riders and spectators. He picked out Roy Gannet in the first row of the grandstand and found Carla nearby. She nodded to him, the cool smile touching her lips, and he tossed her a confident grin as he swung onto the horse. He moved to where Roy Gannet sat and watched the man's eyes go over the palomino.

"Carla said you had an exceptionally fine horse. She was right," Roy said. "If you weren't riding against Owen, you might just win this race."

Canyon smiled and moved away to see Owen Dunstan ride by on the big bay, and he smiled inwardly. The wildness was still there in the horse's eyes, but then, he knew it would be. The bay was more than a horse that disliked its rider; it was also a horse full of barely contained fury. It was a nervous horse, steady only under tight control, and that would be Dunstan's undoing. The man failed to realize his animal's character. Canyon smiled inwardly again. He'd see to it that Dunstan came to that realization. But it would work only if he timed every move perfectly, he knew.

Someone called Ben Stodger's name, and Canyon turned to see a big man in a brown hat and brown shirt, a hard, stony face with a heavy chin. Stodger held his reins with thick-fingered hands, Canyon saw, and his eyes went to the gray gelding Stodger rode. A big, deep-chested horse with plenty of power in rump and forequarters. But its legs were too thin for all that power. They'd tire over a hard course.

"Take your places, gents," the voice called out through a megaphone, and Canyon moved the palomino to the starting line. He took up a position three horses away from Owen Dunstan and saw the man's sneering confidence. Ben Stodger on the big gray was another few horses away, and Canyon's eyes went down the line of riders. Most were on quarter horses with a few thoroughbreds sprinkled among them. Canyon felt the palomino's excitement as the horse caught the tension in the air, the roar of the crowd rolling across the starting line.

"Easy, now, lad," he whispered, and the palomino calmed down. He continued to stroke

Cormac's powerful neck, and the voice came through the megaphone again.

"Ready . . . one . . . two . . . threee-e-e . . ." The shot exploded and drowned out the man's voice. The line of horses surged forward, a wave of pounding hooves.

5

The palomino sprang forward and Canyon let the horse run free for a few moments before firmly pulling back, while most of the other contestants raced on. He saw Owen Dunstan and Ben Stodger had also pulled back on their mounts, and he smiled. Experience showed quickly. Just as he planned, they'd let the overcrowded field thin itself out. The first jump didn't do it, but Canyon watched as the next two jumps came up. He was positioned a dozen yards behind Owen Dunstan and he saw Ben Stodger riding the big gray with easy confidence to his left. The two post-and-rail fences with their deceptive closeness quickly brought down four of the leading riders who'd tried to rush their way over them. Dunstan's big bay took the jumps effortlessly, the man holding the horse in with skilled practice, and Canyon leapt both hurdles with equal ease.

O'Grady stayed behind Dunstan as the hog-back came into sight with its high center rail, and he began to slow his horse as the leaders raced toward the jump with their horses galloping full out, all determined to clear the center rail. He was still holding the palomino back as he watched them jump. Six of them went down on the far side of the barrier, where the ground fell away. Their horses had come down too hard and too fast, and had lost their footing as they landed on the sloping ground. Some of the others managed to stay upright but lost speed and control as their horses fought to retain footing.

Canyon took Cormac over with a tight rein in a controlled jump that landed him on the other side with all four feet well under him, and he was able to handle the ground as it fell away. He let the horse out again as the chicken-coop jump came into view, and he sailed over it with a display of power and horsemanship. He passed two horses in midleap and another two when he hit the ground.

Dunstan and Stodger were still riding easily, O'Grady saw, but he'd closed some distance on Dunstan and saw the man cast a glance back at him. Canyon held his position, and a quick count told him there were some fifteen horses ahead of him as the next post-and-rail jump appeared. He quickly remembered the sharp turn on the other side. He sent the palomino over the jump with plenty of clearance, his hands on the reins ready for the sharp turn. He eased the horse into the curve as a half-dozen riders were yanking back hard on their animals to meet the turn. He swept past another four horses with ease and drew within a dozen yards of Owen Dunstan. This time the man's glance backward held a moment of surprise in it.

The series of twisting, winding curves were next, and Canyon saw Dunstan urge the bay to pick up speed. To his left, Ben Stodger was keeping pace. Canyon let the palomino close a little more as the horse took the curves with easy grace. As the curves ended and led onto a flat straight path, he saw that the leaders were a quartet of quarter horses and a thoroughbred that had shown real speed through the curves.

Canyon's eyes narrowed as he saw the brush-covered stone wall ahead, and he continued to stay back. This was one of the most dangerous of all the jumps, and he saw the lead riders begin to take it too low. Those closest to them made the same mistake, all thinking their horses could push through the brush at the top for an easy jump. As Canyon watched, three of the first riders went down as their mounts hit the stone wall just beneath the brush, the thoroughbred among them. Then four more fell as they were into the jump before they could collect their mounts.

Cormac surged forward, but again Canyon pulled back, saw Dunstan and Ben Stodger clear the barrier with ease, and then he sent the palomino high on the jump and cleared the brush entirely. There were still a half-dozen horses in the lead, but Dunstan decided to move up on them and Canyon followed. Everyone took the hay bale jump with ease, and Canyon was directly behind Dunstan's bay as the brush-and-water jump came into sight. Some of the quarter horses had slowed, he saw, the natural talent and long-legged speed needed to take jump after jump beginning to take its toll. Two riders on good-looking standardbreds appeared to his left, racing from back in the field and riding well.

They settled in close to Bed Stodger's gray and Canyon felt the palomino fighting to surge forward. But he continued to hold the horse in and watched Dunstan take the brush-and-water jump. Three other riders took the jump too short and went down as their mounts hit the water on the other side. Canyon, almost at the barrier, relaxed his grip on the reins and Cormac soared into the air. The horse was stretched full out in the jump and cleared the water before he came down. Canyon saw Dunstan glance back at him, a frown on the man's face this time.

The bay was still going well, though, a talented and powerful horse. But Dunstan hadn't begun to pressure him yet, Canyon smiled inwardly. The strains were still inside the animal, simmering, capable of exploding under the right set of circumstances. Canyon glanced back and saw there were not more than a dozen riders left behind him, plus the half-dozen still ahead. The course had already taken its toll, and he laid a hand alongside the palomino's powerful throat. The horse was still breathing easily, the power in him still there to respond, and Canyon saw the last two double-rail jumps ahead. Dunstan's big bay would take the jumps without trouble, and he'd have the power and speed left for the finish stretch. It was a horse that had won before and could win again, if it were left to breeze along on its own. But Canyon didn't plan to allow that, he reminded himself, and gave the palomino free rein and felt the powerful horse surge forward at once.

Canyon was close at Dunstan's heels as they

neared the next jump, and Dunstan's glance now held a flash of alarm in it as the palomino drew almost abreast of him. Owen took the first double-rail full out, and when he landed, he found Canyon alongside him. Dunstan dug heels into the bay's sides and the horse went forward, but the palomino stayed stride for stride with him.

When they reached the second double-rail jump, Canyon swerved his mount six inches closer to the bay, and both horses took the jump together. But Dunstan touched his riding crop to the bay when they landed and Canyon saw the horse's eyes widen, his head lift, until Dunstan pulled it down. Canyon spurred the palomino forward, swerved again, and came still closer to the bay and watched the horse's eyes roll upward, the wildness flaring in them at once. Canyon took the second set of double-rail jumps almost touching the bay and saw Dunstan having trouble holding his horse under control.

The bay didn't like being closed in, and it liked Dunstan's pressure even less. The wildness in its eyes was coming close to exploding, but Dunstan used the crop again, too insensitive and too much the bully to feel his horse's reactions. The bay surged forward, and Canyon took the palomino with him to go head-to-head over the first triple-rail jump. When they landed, he turned the palomino inward, and the bay veered away only to have its head yanked back. Canyon heard Dunstan's curse.

The last triple-rail was coming up fast, the last rail very high, and Canyon saw the bay's eyes.

The horse was close to bolting. All Dunstan had to do was ease up a little, relax the pressure on the horse, and make up the distance after the jump. But that would be too much for Dunstan's ego, Canyon knew. The jump was but seconds away, and Canyon swerved inward. The bay moved sharply away despite Dunstan's frantic efforts to pull it back. Canyon pulled outward again and took the triple-rail straight on to clear the last, high bar.

He glanced back and saw Dunstan trying to bring his horse around at the last moment, but the bay was fighting him now, eyes wild and nostrils flaring. Dunstan still pressed, unable or unwilling to realize his horse couldn't be pressed past a certain point. The bay wouldn't try to please its rider with a last, valiant effort. It was a horse filled with anger that exploded instead of responding, and Owen Dunstan had made it that way. As the palomino landed, Canyon saw Dunstan, unable to straighten the bay out, take the jump at an angle, and the horse's hind legs hit the last high bar. Somehow, it managed not to go down, but with eyes rolled back in its head and slavering foam flying from its mouth, the bay yanked its head sideways, half-bucked, and almost threw Dunstan.

Canyon heard Dunstan's shouts of fury as he fought to bring the horse under control. He'd do so, Canyon knew, but when he did, he'd be at least a dozen lengths behind and the bay would never make it up for him. Canyon glanced to his left to see Ben Stodger on the big gray going all out as the horses pounded onto the straight, wide path of the finishing stretch. But the gray's legs were coming down too stiff and hard, and Canyon saw that the horse was running on the last of its strength. Canyon slapped his hand lightly against Cormac's neck and felt the horse respond. But he heard the harsh breathing in the powerful throat: the race had taken its toll on every horse. He eased the horse back. He was two lengths ahead of Stodger and saw the gray fall back another length. The others who were still left were far back, and he grunted in satisfaction as he saw Dunstan still fighting with the bay.

The finish line was only a dozen yards away now, and Canyon let the palomino cross it in long, powerful strides without urging more from the horse. As the roar of the crowd filled the air, he crossed the line four lengths ahead of Ben Stodger and gently pulled back on the reins, letting the horse slow and go into a canter at the far end of the track. He turned the horse, moved into a trot, and rode back to the grandstand. He brought the horse to a walk alongside the long benches and saw the compact figure of Carla Gannet stand up, nod to him with a slow smile, and turn away to disappear into the crowds.

Canyon rode on to where a man waited at the center of the grandstand with a large, ornate, heavy silver trophy. He saw Roy Gannet step up beside the man. Canyon halted, let the palomino blow his nostrils clear, and moved toward the two men. His eyes found Carla and he saw her watching him, her face carefully composed as he tossed her a wide grin. She allowed no expression to touch her face.

He halted before Roy Gannet. "Congratulations, O'Grady," the man said. "The Missouri Challenge Cup trophy is yours." The other man handed the heavy cup to him and he gathered it in with one arm. "You're the first outsider who's ever won this," Gannet said.

"Doesn't surprise me," Canyon said. He turned the horse and halted in front of Carla. "I think it should stay here," he said. "I present it to Miss Carla Gannet." Carla's smile was polite but nothing more as he handed the trophy to her and wheeled the palomino in a tight circle. He saw Owen Dunstan standing beside his horse, the man's face flushed with anger, his lips tight.

Ben Stodger sat the gray nearby, and the man moved toward him. "A fine ride, mister," he said. "My name's Ben Stodger. I could use a man like you if you're in need of a job. Fact is, six of my men just left."

"Is that so? Just walked out on you?" Canyon asked mildly.

"Yep, just up and disappeared," Stodger said, and Canyon took in the answer, filing it in a corner of his mind.

"Maybe I'll come visit," Canyon said, and moved on, to find Owen Dunstan blocking his path.

"You won only because that damn bay acted up at the last minute," the man said.

"He acted up because you don't know anything about handling a horse," Canyon said, the words a sharp contrast to the affability of his voice, and Owen Dunstan's face clouded.

"You're still a peasant, O'Grady. Winning hasn't changed that any," Dunstan snapped.

"You're still an arrogant ass. Losing hasn't taught you anything," Canyon returned. Dunstan turned and strode away, but the hate in his eyes wouldn't vanish, Canyon knew. He slowly rode and halted before Carla as she walked with the trophy in her arms. Her black eyes gave him a sidelong glance.

"Thank you for the trophy," she said. "A charming gesture."

"I'll be stopping by to see my trophy," Canyon said.

"Which one?" she slid at him tartly as she hurried away, and he let his chuckle follow her. He ran his hand down across the palomino's throat, reached down to the powerful shoulder. The horse's coat was damp with flecks of sweat, and Canyon rode slowly from the crowds, moved up a gentle hill in the afternoon sun, and halted at the top. He dismounted, unsaddled the horse, and let the mount roam freely while the sun dried him off.

Canyon shed some of his clothes and stretched out on a bed of sweet clover, let his muscles relax, and dozed until the sun vanished over the distant hills and the cool twilight wind woke him. He dressed, let the night come over the land, and finally saddled the palomino again to slowly make his way to town and the Dry Corner Kitten. The bartender called out a greeting when he entered, and Canyon waved back, made his way to a corner table, and ordered a whiskey. One of the girls brought it, lingered to see if she could interest him in something more, and finally wandered away.

He sat alone through another drink and had almost finished it when a figure approached. He saw a man in a black jacket and tan trousers, a wide collar with a string tie hanging loosely from the neck. Canyon took in a mild face, rimless glasses sitting high on a straight nose, light-blue eyes that gazed at him from a face that was remarkable only for its ordinariness.

"Mind if I sit down for a few minutes?" the man asked, a glass of whiskey in his hand.

"No." Canyon nodded.

"You fit the description of the man who won the race this morning."

"I do and I am."

"Congratulations. I'm Ben Burton," the man said.

"Canyon O'Grady. I take it you weren't at the race."

"No, had an emergency call. It happens when you're the only dentist for miles around," Ben Burton said. "This is a state that's full of emergencies."

Canyon felt his fingers tighten around the glass, and he formed his answer carefully, the words committed to memory. "It's a place where a man can find whatever he wants to find," he said, and drained the last of the whiskey in his glass as he waited.

"And a lot he'd rather not find," Burton said, and Canyon set the glass down and met the light-blue eyes that gazed mildly out at him from behind the rimless glasses. He nodded and saw the faint smile touch the man's lips. "Let's walk," he said, and Ben rose with him.

"I'll show you my office," Burton said. "It's only a few streets down."

Canyon waved to the bartender as he followed the dentist outside, unhitched the palomino, and led the horse down the street with him until Ben halted at a narrow frame building, took out a key, and went inside.

Canyon draped the reins over a mailbox and followed the man into a small, neat office. A dentist's chair sat in the center and the flowered wallpaper on the walls seemed more faded than it was in the low lamplight.

Ben Burton gestured to a hard-backed chair as he slid onto the leather of the dentist's chair.

"You surprised me," Canyon said. "I never thought they'd pick the town dentist for a contact man."

"You hear a lot out of a dentist's chair. Men get nervous when they come here, and they tend to talk," Burton said. "The right questions can bring out a lot of information. Besides, nobody ever figures a dentist for anything but fixing toothaches."

"I know the outlines. Give me the details."

"Roy Gannet's spending a lot of money to be elected Senator," the man began. "He has his admirers, but they're mostly big ranchers and money people. My information has it that most of the smaller farmers and settlers in the outlying districts relate better to Hal Colbert, and they lean toward voting for him. But Roy Gannet's been sending strong-arm squads all over the countryside, threatening, beating up on people, doing a real job of terror and intimidation.''

"Washington feels it may be succeeding," Canyon said.

"That's right. Besides these strong-arm tactics, many of the loans these small farmers have are with banks Gannet controls. Many sell to outlets he operates, and many depend on outfits he owns for their supplies.''

"What's Colbert doing to get votes?"

"He makes speeches, talks about the plans he has for the people. He puts up posters, which Gannet instantly pastes over with his own,'' the dentist said. "As I said, people like him, but Gannet's power and bully tactics are scaring folks. All he has to do is scare them enough so they vote for him or don't vote at all.''

"What else can you tell me about Hal Colbert?"

"There's not a lot anybody knows about him. He moved here a few years back, made friends with a lot of small farmers. He doesn't do a lot of ranching, but he seems to have money. I hear it comes from old family connections,'' Ben Burton said.

"Then the first thing is to stop Gannet's strong-arm tactics,'' Canyon thought aloud.

"Easier said than done. On the surface, his squads come on as campaign workers for him, and there's no law against that. Then they do the strong-arm stuff undercover and leave it to the people to make the connection, which isn't hard to do. So far, there's no real proof they've ever done anything wrong.''

"Then we'll have to get some proof," Canyon said. "Anybody ever confront Gannet with this?"

"Not around here. As I said, he swings a lot of power." Ben Burton paused, his face folded itself into a frown and he shook his head almost sadly. "Funny thing is that Roy Gannet's a likable man. He likes being rich and he likes his rich friends. He wants to be senator, but that's no crime of itself, and I've never heard of him doing anything to hurt anybody until he began to run for senator."

"The thirst for power has a way of making a man forget everything else," Canyon said. "It's time to put an end to Roy Gannet's methods. Washington feels he's tied to the slave-state interests. If we could get proof of that, we'd have him."

"Proof? How?" Burton asked.

"Find one of those ties," Canyon said. "Tell me about Owen Dunstan."

"Roy Gannet's right-hand man, but he's no Roy Gannet. He's mean where Gannet's forceful, cruel where Gannet's strong, and just plain evil where Gannet's ruthless. But he carries out orders."

"What about Carla Gannet?"

"Gannet dotes on her. She's smart enough to pull strings behind the scenes," the dentist said.

"And the other daughter?"

"Bad blood between her and Gannet. Details have been hushed up, but it goes deep," Burton said.

"I'll find out more about that on my own."

"The folks in Dryad County, just north of here, are holding a county meeting in a few days, I'm told. They'll be talking about the election, you can be sure. Maybe we ought to look in. You might see Gannet's squads at work firsthand," the dentist said.

"Good. Get the details and I'll be in touch," Canyon agreed.

"I live here behind the office, so you can most always find me here. No one's going to think anything of your visiting the dentist at any hours. Folks do it all the time," Ben said.

"Now I see why Washington picked you as a contact," Canyon said as he rose and went to the door. Ben Burton let him out and he climbed onto the palomino. A sharp, alert mind lurked behind Ben Burton's very ordinary visage, he decided as he rode through the darkened streets of Dry Corn. He rode into the low hills, found a spot to bed down and undressed. It'd take Burton a few days to pin down the information he needed. Meanwhile there were other avenues to pursue, with promises of more pleasure . . . Canyon smiled as he fell to sleep.

6

When O'Grady woke, the morning sun had come over the horizon to fling a warm cloak across the land. He found a tiny pond, not much more than a sinkhole, but it was filled with fresh water. He washed and dressed. When he finished, he had decided to pay his first call on Glenda. Perhaps anger and bitterness would loosen her tongue. There was certainly enough of it inside her, he had come to realize. Yet, beneath it, she was warm, with her own hints of promise. She was probably more complex than Carla, Canyon mused as he rode toward her place. But then Carla had probably never needed more than her striking beauty.

He turned off further idle musings as he reached Glenda's spread, rode in, and saw Tad Elkins grooming one of the Kabardine mares. The man waved at him as he halted before the main house.

Glenda appeared in the doorway, the red-checked skirt resting on the high line of her breasts, the top three buttons open and the smooth, swelling curves beautifully visible. A tiny line of perspiration crossed her forehead and she wiped it away with the back of her sleeve. "Just finished feeding chores," she said. "Got some cold bohea. Come in and have some."

Canyon nodded and followed her into the house where she poured a glass of strong, dark tea for him and for herself. Her combination of tomboy and very compact femaleness created its own appeal, he decided, a kind of raucous sensuousness.

"I wondered if you'd be stopping by today," Glenda said.

"Why?"

"I thought you'd be visiting someone else," she said.

"Such as Carla." He smiled and her half-shrug was an admission.

"She had something to do with you deciding to race," Glenda said.

"You're guessing."

"No, I know her."

"But you don't know me. I raced because I wanted to win," he said.

"For a trophy you didn't want and gave back." Glenda laughed. "There had to be more. What'd she promise you?"

"She didn't promise me anything," Canyon said firmly. The answer wasn't a lie, he told himself. A wager wasn't a promise. "Besides, I didn't stop by to talk about Carla. You've things you didn't finish explaining," he said. "Tell me about your husband."

He saw Glenda's eyes grow narrow and the anger come into her face. "Father never wanted me to marry Jim," she said. "Jim was wild, no good, reckless. He only wanted me for my inheritance, according to father.''

"Was it true?" Canyon asked.

"I never thought so. I never got the chance to find out.''

"But you went and married him. To spite your pa?" Canyon probed.

"Maybe some of that was in it," she admitted. "But Jim was handsome and dashing and full of wonderful wildness. He loved risking his neck. He loved riding a horse through the dead of night as fast as he could. He loved trying to ride a bronco without a saddle.''

"Is that how he was killed?''

"That's what they said. It was the second night of our marriage. He'd gone off to ride alone. It gave him more energy, he said, got all his juices going. I waited and he never came back. They found him in the morning where he'd fallen off the edge of a ravine.''

"What makes you think that's not just what happened?" Canyon frowned.

"Daddy was livid when I married Jim. He told me the marriage wouldn't last a week. He saw to it. Jim would never have fallen off the edge of a ravine. He was too good a rider. I went to the spot. There was no sign his horse had slipped, no marks on the ground to show that. He'd been ambushed and thrown over.''

"Just because there were no marks of the horse slipping at the edge of the ravine? That's not enough to build a case on, lass," Canyon said.

"There was something else. I looked around the spot on my own. I found half of one of the cigarettes Daddy smokes. He's the only one who smokes them. He rolls his own," she said, her eyes meeting Canyon's stare with hurt inside their anger.

O'Grady let his lips purse in thought. "You go to the sheriff and tell him what you thought?"

"The sheriff owes his job to Daddy," she snorted.

"There was a road alongside the ravine, I take it," Canyon said, and she nodded. "Your father could've ridden that way a day earlier and tossed that half a cigarette there. You don't have real proof. You're trying to fit things together."

"It's proof enough for me," Glenda snapped, icy fury in her voice. "I know my father. I know how he doesn't like to be crossed."

She was certain of her conclusions, Canyon saw, no give in her voice, not the slightest room for doubt. "How does all this fit in with you thinking your father tried to burn you out the other night?"

"It doesn't, except as one more example of the kind of man he is," Glenda said. "He wanted me to use part of my inheritance to help him win the election as senator. Instead, I went and bought all my stock and set up my breeding operation here. He wants to force me to quit and come home and help him win the election. He likes to force people to do what he wants. He can't stand being crossed." She came toward him and closed her arms around him and suddenly she was all soft and warm. There was a lost-child appeal to her.

"If you're right, I'm sorry for you, and there's

nothing can change the past. But if you're not, I'm sorry you think you are, and maybe something can be done about that," he said.

"I'm right," she murmured with unswerving certainty and he pulled back to offer a wry smile.

"Seems to me you'll not be pulling for your father," he said.

"You can count on that. I'd vote for Hal Colbert," she said.

"You know Hal Colbert?"

"We've met. He's a good man. He deserves to be elected," she said, but offered nothing more to put meat on her words.

"So I've heard," Canyon said blandly. Washington agreed with her, he commented inwardly. "I hear your daddy's campaign methods are on the rough side. What do you know about them?"

"Not a lot. But I've heard the same thing."

"You know about his routine, his associates such as Owen Dunstan. Anything would help," Canyon said.

"Help what?" she asked, eyes narrowing at once, and he grimaced inwardly. "Who are you, Canyon O'Grady?"

He'd been careless and had picked the wrong phrase. "Someone who wants to help you," he answered quickly. "If you're right about your father, you deserve help, and he deserves to be stopped."

"Doing good deeds again?" she slid back.

"Why not?" He smiled. "I didn't do badly for you so far. I can do more. It's habit-forming."

Her mouth came to his, soft yet with controlled firmness. "Yes, thank you," she said. "But I can't talk now, not with all the chores waiting."

"I'll come by tomorrow night," Canyon said, and she nodded.

"Good. We can talk them," she said, and held her hand in his as he walked outside to the palomino.

He watched her wave at him as he rode off, and when he finally was out of her sight, he let a deep breath of air blow from his lips. He had managed to make a recovery, but he'd have to be more careful, he grunted. It would take little bits and pieces to get to Roy Gannet, and he'd pursue every avenue. Glenda was certainly one, and she was turning out to be a surprising package of complexities. But perhaps she'd be the key to stopping Roy Gannet. She was certainly filled with enough dark currents to pursue. But Carla was closest to her father and she was still the best place to start, he told himself.

He rode through the countryside until the Gannet ranch came into sight, looking larger than it had by night. He saw Roy Gannet beside a fence with Owen Dunstan, and Roy looked up from his conversation to wave. Canyon walked the palomino to where the two men were, and saw Dunstan's eyes were made of icy disdain. Losing hadn't taken any of the arrogance out of him, Canyon noted silently.

"Carla told me you might drop by, said she wanted to show you the place," Roy Gannet boomed.

"That's right." Canyon smiled. Carla thought

quickly, he laughed inwardly. Reasons hastily put into place to fend off questions. More for her sake than his, he was certain.

"I'd show you around myself, but Owen and I have some campaign plans to go over," Roy said. "This campaign takes a lot of time. You can't miss any chance to influence the voters."

"Guess not," Canyon said pleasantly, and moved on to the house as the two men returned to their conversation.

The tall small-waisted figure came from the house as he dismounted, jet-black hair falling loosely against a white silk blouse that clung deliciously to the long curve of her breasts.

"I hear you offered to show me the ranch," Canyon said, his snapping blue eyes carrying their own message. "Did you think I needed an excuse to come visit?"

"I thought it might help," Carla said evenly, her face carefully composed.

"Then let's go through the motions," Canyon said, and drew a narrowed glance. He followed her to the first of the corrals.

"Part of our Herefords, the best in the state," Carla said as she leaned on the corral fence and her black skirt moved with a light breeze to outline the long curve of her thighs.

Canyon brought his eyes back to the herd and nodded appreciatively. They were all fine specimens, well-kept and in top condition. She led him to an adjoining corral where a large herd of saddle horses ran free. Most were browns and bays, some Morgan stock mixed in with thoroughbred and perhaps a little quarter horse, he noted.

"Daddy's riding stock. He sells to ranches back East for top dollar," Carla said, and he followed her through the stables, where she took pride in pointing out the roomy stalls, solid wood construction, and well-kept airiness. "Daddy feels that a well-kept horse is a happy horse, and a happy horse is easy to manage."

"He's right," Canyon agreed, and saw the big bay alone in a corner stall. "Except for that one," he murmured.

"Owen hasn't gone near him since the race," she said. "I think Daddy suggested he let the horse alone for a while."

Canyon followed her out of the stables into the space alongside the next corral, where he saw some dozen or so horses. Some hobbled about on knobby knees, a few peacefully nibbled on a bale of hay, others leaned gray-whiskered snouts against the fence, and a few trotted slowly around the corral. They all had one thing in common, he saw: all were old and far past their prime, yet they were as well-tended as the fine saddle horses.

"The old-timers," Carla said.

Canyon questioned with a frown, and she let a soft smile break the careful stiffness she'd kept in her face.

"They're all old horses we've had. Most ranchers would sell them off for slaughter or put them down. Daddy won't do that. He feels they've earned the right to live out their lives in comfort. He does that with all the older stock,'' Carla explained.

Canyon felt the surprise curl inside him. It was something that didn't fit what he'd heard about Roy Gannet. "A very nice thing, really nice," he said, and glanced up to see Roy Gannet and Dunstan riding from the ranch together.

"I guess we can stop the pretending now," Carla said, and he caught the glimmer of harshness in the black eyes. "Where?" she said.

"You could sound a little less grim," he observed mildly.

"I'm sorry. I didn't mean to sound that way," she apologized. "I'm just not used to this kind of thing."

"You mean losing bets?"

"Losing this kind of bet."

"I'll take a room in town."

"Too many people might recognize me in Dry Corn. Even by night." Carla paused, and he caught the tiny smile that touched her lips. "Besides, I like to be relaxed," she said. "Father and Owen are leaving for a few days, campaign work. I'll be alone tonight."

"No, you won't," Canyon said.

"I'll leave the light on in my room. Come to the window. I'll let you in the side door. An hour after dark."

"My pleasure," Canyon said with a bow that she accepted with a half-curtsy.

"Two can play at being gallant, Canyon O'Grady," she said.

"No playing at it at all, my beautiful Carla. I may have won, but I'm still honored," he said, and she made no further reply as she walked to the palomino with him. He saw her watching him from the ranch, black eyes narrowed with speculation, and he turned the horse east toward Dry Corn, aware that he had begun to view the evening ahead with definite anticipation.

The afternoon was nearing an end when he rode into town and dismounted outside Ben Burton's office. He had to wait till the dentist finished with a patient, and when he did, Burton quickly closed his office door. "The Dryad County meeting will be held two nights from now at the old granary shed. I know the place. It's often used for county meetings and square dances. We'll go together," Burton said. "Be here at seven."

"Good," Canyon said, and quickly left to see that night had already fallen. He left town, wandered across the low hills, and found the Gannet spread still and dark when he reached it, except for the lone light from a curtained window in the left wing of the house.

Canyon rode to the window, dismounted, and saw Carla draw aside the curtain to peer out and then vanish. He heard the door open, followed the sound, and found her waiting, her slender shape encased in a full-length blue silk robe. She led him to her room and he stepped inside. It was all done in pink: pink sheets on the bed at one side, pink pillows, pink-flowered wallpaper, pink coverings on the dresser and a stuffed chair. It made for a very feminine, delicate room that was strangely restful to the eye. It did one thing more, he observed: it made Carla Gannet's jet-black hair and alabaster skin even more striking as she stood against the warm, delicate pink.

She faced him, stood very straight, her black eyes veiled. No grimness to her now, but something else, a kind of defiance, he decided.

"You make it terribly hard to leave, lass." He smiled.

"Leave?" Carla echoed, a tiny furrow crossing the pure white of her brow.

"Yes, I won't be holding you to your wager." He smiled again and saw the furrow become a frown.

"You mean that?"

"I do," he said ruefully. "Take it as proof that gentleman is just another word for damn fool."

"Why are you doing this?"

"Some things can't be won. They must be given freely," he said. He tossed her another wide smile. "I'll be leaving now before I come to my senses." He started to turn from her.

"No, you can't," Carla said, and he turned back in surprise.

"I can't?"

"Gambling debts are debts of honor. Surely you know that."

"That's true," Canyon agreed.

"I won't go back on a debt of honor, and it's wrong of you to ask that."

Canyon allowed himself to consider her words for a moment, and he kept the smile inside himself. He had expected some reaction from her, and it was better than he'd hoped for. But his face was serious as he looked at her. "I suppose it is, now that you put it that way," he said, and unhooked his gun belt and let it drop to the floor. "Then it's time for paying up."

Carla's black eyes were suddenly smoldering coals, he saw, and with one hand she undid the belt of the robe. The garment fell open, and he glimpsed the pure white curve of one long thigh. Then she moved her shoulders, a graceful, fluid motion, and the robe slid from her to fall in folds at her feet. Canyon heard the low gasp that fell from his lips as she stood beautifully naked in front of him.

"I think of Blake. 'The nakedness of woman is the work of God,' he said. He was right," Canyon murmured.

He let his eyes take in the magnificence of her body, tall and slender, yet not at all frail. Shoulders a little thin, but the longish breasts curved beautifully in a slow line that grew full at the bottoms, where the cups turned upwards. Against her alabaster skin, the tiny pink nipples seemed fiery, the pink circle around each glowing. He took in a narrow waist that curved into fairly wide hips, an absolutely flat belly, and the tangled hirsute triangle was a patch as jet as the hair that fell to her shoulders. Below it, long, slow-curving thighs were as beautifully white and long as the petals of jasmine.

Carla waited, her eyes never leaving him as he tore off his clothes and stepped to her, his hand curling around the back of her neck. She came forward, her lips opening at once, her mouth on his, her tongue finding his at once. He half-lifted, half-swung her onto the bed, and she pushed sideways, turned him onto his back, and let her eyes move down his muscled symmetry. He felt himself rising at once as her hands moved along the skin, her touch soft yet firm.

"Oh, oh, my," Carla breathed, and brought one alabaster thigh half across his groin, rubbing her leg back and forth on him. Her mouth came down on his again, and he reached up and cupped one breast in his hand, let his thumb move slowly back and forth across the tiny pink tip, and felt it rise, grow firm, and beckon.

Canyon brought his lips to its tiny point, pulled gently, caressed, let his tongue trace a circle around its soft edges, and he heard Carla cry out in pleasure as her hands tightened against him. "Oh, oh, God . . . ooooh," she cried out, her velvet voice a notch lower and covered with a soft huskiness.

He drew the alabaster mound deeper into his mouth, and she half-moaned. Her hands pressed against his chest, moved down to his abdomen, and met his own hand, which slid downward and pressed gently against her flat belly, pushing into the black tangle that covered the little rise of her pubic mound. His hand smoothed, pressed, and caressed, and Carla's moans were low soft songs that circled the room. When his hands dropped lower to trace invisible lines along the insides of her thighs, she cried out in purring anticipation.

"Yes, yes, oh, oh, oh my God . . ." Carla breathed as she half-twisted her hips. Her thighs fell open, then came together again, her knees rising, stretching out, rising again, every part of her body seeking, asking, offering, the language of the limbs. He brought himself slowly over her, rested against the curly triangle, and Carla half-screamed in delight. He felt her legs lift again, thighs close around his hips, and he rose enough to let his throbbing gift rest against her lubricious lips, moist and warm, pulsating with welcome. His lips closed over one longish breast as he slid forward, and Carla screamed, a cry of pure pleasure as her arms clasped around his back and pulled him forward.

"Yes, oh, yes . . . more, oh, more, Canyon . . . more," Carla Gannet whispered in low, breathy gasps that rose in pitch as he obeyed until words became a sing-song moan of desire and delight. She held back nothing, letting her sensuous warmth translate into hip-writhing motions, the body becoming supreme, the power of the flesh above all else.

She moved with him, hips twisting, writhing, using every bit of her encasing warmth to hold him, rub with him, contract, and send the sensations of ecstasy to new heights. All the while she moaned in her low, husky sound. Suddenly, yet without harsh abruptness, her body tightened and her sensuous thrustings were carried on new surges, her entire torso stretching, contracting, surging again. Her cry, when it came, seemed to be torn from the very depths of her, the low, husky voice growing in strength, rising in pitch, then finally bursting forth in a scream that embraced ecstasy and defeat, fulfillment and dismay, eternity and evanescence, all and nothing.

She held in midair for a last desperate, clinging moment and then collapsed under him, a low, half-sobbing cry murmured against his chest, and he lay half atop her, the aftermath of his own ecstasy evident as he gasped in deep breaths of air.

He finally pushed onto one elbow and took in the real beauty of her, heightened by the delicate contrast of colors, her alabaster whiteness against the pink sheets, her raven's-wing hair a black halo. She lay in languorous loveliness, one leg stretched out, the other half-drawn up, breasts falling gracefully to one side, and she was plainly very much aware of herself. She reached one hand up, moved it across his chest, and pulled him down to lay against her.

"Are you going to tell me who you are, Canyon O'Grady?" she murmured. "And what brought you here?"

Questions of idle curiosity? He smiled inwardly. Or sharp probes hidden in the warm languor of intimacy? "But I have, lass," he said with mild protest, and saw her smile back.

"Fairy tales, you've told me, Canyon," she said.

"Fairy tales are always better than the reality of this world. Princes are always handsome, maidens in distress are always beautiful, and everyone lives happily ever after."

"You're telling me to be content with your fairy tale," she said. "I can't be. I'm just more curious because of it."

He reached over and kissed her, and her lips responded at once. "A little curiosity is good for one," he murmured, and she drew back, her black eyes studying him.

"The question is, are you good for one?" Carla remarked.

He smiled back. She could use words layered with meanings. Beauty and brains to match. He found himself wondering if she had used her beauty with calculation or abandon. If she had started with the first, she'd ended with the second, he was certain, and he could have no complaint there.

"What about Carla Gannet?" he asked. "Is she excited at the prospect of being a senator's daughter?"

"I guess so."

"You help on the campaign trail?" Canyon questioned casually.

"Behind the scenes, mostly. I plan strategy."

"I hear your father is waging a hard campaign."

"Daddy believes in winning," Carla said, and turned on her stomach, her long, tight rear a gorgeous curve of pure white.

"There's winning and there's browbeating people into voting for you," Canyon answered.

Her frown was instant. "You've been listening to those stories. They're lies, all of them," Carla said. "Or did little Glenda tell you that?"

"No, she didn't. You two don't get along, do you?" he said. "Did you ever?"

"A little, when Mother was alive. She handled Glenda by just giving into her all the time. When she died, little Glenda couldn't get her way anymore," Carla said. "That's when she started hating Daddy and blaming him for everything. Glenda has real problems now."

Canyon smiled soothingly. "It wasn't because you were your father's favorite, was it?"

"She was jealous of that all the time," Carla said. "She made herself such a bitch that nobody wanted her around."

Canyon smiled inwardly. Two sisters, two very different stories. Only one could be true. Thoughts snapped off as Carla turned and reached arms around him.

"No more talk about campaigns or Glenda," she said, and pressed herself against him, all pure, unblemished softness as her mouth found his.

"You satisfied that debt of honor. You can't use the same excuse twice," Canyon said laconically.

She pulled back and he found a black-eyed stare blazing at him. He smiled affably. "Your gallantry has deserted you, it seems," she hissed.

"Everyone's entitled to an occasional lapse," he said mildly, and her lips softened into a hint of a smile.

"All right, no excuses anymore. Just eagerness. Is that honest enough?"

"Honesty deserves rewarding," he said, cupped one breast, and brought his lips to the tiny pink tip.

Carla's low, husky moan rose up at once. Canyon smiled and felt himself reaching for her, pulsating, searching. Once again the night became a thing of lithe, surging sensuousness until finally he was one with her, and her cries spiraled through the room.

He lay beside her until dawn came, and he knew her alabaster beauty against the pink sheets would remain imprinted in his mind. He dressed and she rose, draped the robe loosely around her, and walked to the door with him.

"Daddy will be making more campaign trips," Carla Gannet said. "Stop by and keep informed."

"Definitely," he said as he left.

7

He slept well past the early morning under the generous shade of a red oak, and when he woke, he lay on the bedroll and let the night return. It was wonderful even in the shadowed world of rememberings. Carla had said little that was revealing about her father, but she had admitted a hand in planning his campaign, and her defense of it had been quick. Was she pulling the strings from behind the scene as Ben Burton had suggested might well be the case? It was possible, Canyon realized as he finally rose, washed, and leisurely dressed.

He decided to do some scouting on his own, and he rode back to the Gannet place, approached from one side, and halted beneath a cluster of thick bitternut that let him see the entire ranch.

Roy Gannet had returned, he saw as he watched the man move around his ranch, confer with a man who seemed to be his foreman. Carla appeared in dungarees and a tight-fitting, light-blue shirt that clung to her breasts as she carried two buckets of oats into the corral where the old horses were cloistered. Canyon watched as Roy

Gannet entered the corral after her. The man paused to stroke each one of the old horses before disappearing into the stable while Carla finished the feeding.

Perhaps Roy Gannet was a man of many personalities, Canyon pondered. Owen Dunstan didn't appear, and finally Carla vanished into the house and her father soon after. Nothing out of the ordinary happened at the ranch.

Canyon finally rode away in the afternoon sun. He'd gone about a half-mile when he spotted the two buckboards stopped on the road below. He moved closer and saw that each carried a sign that read VOTE FOR HAL COLBERT.

He moved down to the road, and Canyon saw each carried a stack of flyers.

"Take one, friend," the man in the first buckboard called out, and Canyon picked a flyer from the stack. It urged readers to vote for Hal Colbert with the usual overblown slogans common to such flyers.

"Going to distribute these, I take it," Canyon said.

"Yep, I'm going east and Zeb, there, he's going west. We've probably got enough for three towns each," the man said. "It ought to take all of today and tomorrow."

"Colbert doing anything more than passing out flyers?" Canyon asked.

"Personal campaigning. He's at a gathering of local folks at the Bensen place. It's only fifteen minutes from here. You could make it if you've a mind to," the man said.

"Thanks, I'll do that," Canyon said, and sent

the palomino off in a canter as the two buckboards rolled on. He found the Bensen place along the same road, the barn strung with colored ribbons and campaign posters. He dismounted and entered the barn to find some twenty-five people listening to Hal Colbert, who had climbed onto a bale of hay and had already begun his speech.

"Roy Gannet cares only about power. I care about you, the small farmers and small ranchers. If you elect Roy Gannet, you'll be dancing to his tune, mark my words," Hal Colbert said. "Just look at how he's trying to strong-arm you good people into voting for him."

"A lot of us depend on Roy Gannet's banks and his companies. It's hard to turn your back on that," a man answered.

"But you have to. That's the only way you can get free of him. Elect me and I'll see to your interests," Colbert said.

"Where do you stand on keeping Missouri a free state?" someone called out.

"I stand with you on that," Colbert said.

Canyon frowned inwardly. It was a politician's answer, the question turned around rather than answered. He felt a stab of disappointment in Hal Colbert. He'd expected more of the man, even though he knew that office-seekers were the same everywhere. He quickly returned his attention to Colbert.

"Roy Gannet's trying to scare you, force you, intimidate you. Vote for me and answer him." Colbert finished to applause that was more polite than enthusiastic.

The crowd began to drift off in small groups, and Canyon saw Colbert approach him.

"An unexpected pleasure, Canyon O'Grady. You decide to come work for me?" the man asked, his mild, thin face allowing a glimmer of hope.

"Sorry, just passing by," Canyon said. "How's it going?"

"We're doing our best, but it's hard. Roy Gannet's leaning real hard on people. We're just trying to get our message out," Colbert said. He let a smile break the slightly pinched seriousness of his face. "You file that you're planning to settle in the northern part of the state, and we can get you registered to vote."

"Sorry, can't say that. But I'll be rooting for you." Canyon smiled.

"My offer's still open, O'Grady. Come work for me anytime," Colbert said.

"I'll keep remembering that," Canyon said.

"Just what brought you to these parts? I never did find that out," Colbert said.

"Nothing special. Happened to wind up here in my wandering."

Colbert allowed another smile behind the rimless glasses. "I guess we're all wanderers, O'Grady," he said as he walked away with two men at his heels.

Colbert was suspicious of his answer, Canyon realized. But, then, that wasn't unusual. Most people didn't accept his reply at face value.

Canyon left the barn and climbed onto the palomino as the others had begun to go their own ways. He rode slowly across the darkening dusk to Dry Corn, stopped at the saloon, and had a sandwich as night descended.

When he rode past Ben Burton's house, he saw the light on in the rear, but he continued out of town and rode across the low hills. He reached Glenda's place and dismounted outside the front door as she emerged, her round, compact figure silhouetted by the light behind her.

"Is that what she promised you if you won?" he heard her hiss, and he saw the fury in her face as she stepped closer.

"What are you talking about?" He frowned.

"You know what I'm talking about. Carla. She promised you a night in bed if you won the race," Glenda flung at him. "Well, you can go back for some more."

He felt the surprise stab at him and fell back on his original evasion. "Carla didn't promise me anything for winning, I told you that."

"You just spent the night with her, dammit," Glenda snapped.

"Now, what makes you think I did that?"

"Don't add lies to it, Canyon O'Grady," Glenda said, and managed to look hurt as well as furious.

He let answers race through his mind, discarded most as they flew by. He had offered her help. He had to stay with the role he'd made for himself. "You're singing the right tune but the wrong words, lass," he said.

"Don't try to fancy-talk me," she blazed. "Say what you mean, Canyon O'Grady."

"I spent the night at Carla's. I went there to help you."

"That's dipping deep into your bag of fairy tales," Glenda frowned, skepticism clouding her face.

"Look, you think your father killed your husband of one day. You think he tried to burn you out. I said I'd help you find the truth. I'd like to see a fair campaign. It seemed to me that if I could get Carla talking, I might learn something to help."

Glenda's eyes stayed fastened on him, her brow furrowed. "Did you?" she thrust.

"Some. Not enough. It was a start."

"All from just talk?"

"Talk, fencing with words, playing games."

"I'll bet."

He ignored her barb. "I came tonight to see if you'd have more to say, something that might help. That's how I'll find the truth, if it can be found."

She held him with her appraising stare. "I might believe that all you did was talk, but for only one reason."

"And what might that be?" he questioned.

"Carla's too high and mighty just to fall into bed with anyone, even a handsome rogue such as yourself," Glenda muttered.

"You know your sister," Canyon said, letting ruefulness cross his face while he breathed a silent sigh of relief. "Now, may I come in? We have some more talking to do." He started forward, but the palm of her hand came up to press against his chest.

"No," she said firmly. "Not tonight. I want

some time to think some more about you, and this and your fine words."

He shrugged. "Whatever you say," he answered. He knew better than to push. Her initial fury had retreated. That was victory enough for the moment. He had salvaged the best he could out of it for now. He turned and pulled himself onto the bronzed horse. "I'll be coming by again," he said, and making no reply, she let her shoulders lift in a half-shrug before she turned and strode into the house, round, full little rear straining the seat of the Levi's she wore.

He rode away with one question burning inside him. He hadn't dared ask it, of course, and he'd not have received an answer if he had. How did she know about his night with Carla? Had someone seen him leave and told her? People liked carrying tales. Or had someone been watching the Gannet house through the night? Had Colbert decided to make his own countermoves? Had Glenda been out riding and seen him herself? He grimaced at the thought. It was damned unlikely at that hour, yet he couldn't rule out the possibility. Perhaps she had hired someone to watch her father's house and report to her. That would explain her knowing. Yet it didn't sit right. She had the hate for it, the determination also. But, why now, all of a sudden? Because of the attempt to burn down her house? That could account for it, he reasoned as he brought his thoughts back to the present. Speculation answered nothing, but action might, he told himself as he turned the palomino north across the low hillside.

A half-moon hung high in the blue velvet sky

when he neared the Gannet ranch. He drew a little closer and then dismounted, the horse ground-tied, and went forward on foot. There were plenty of places from which to watch Roy Gannet's spread, some closer than others, but all afforded a clear view. He'd used one only a few hours earlier, he reminded himself as he crept to the top of a low hill and stayed in a line of tall bush. The ranch lay below, the buildings dark except for a night lamp at the stable door. His gaze traveled slowly across the nearest line of trees and peered deep into the shadows, but he found nothing and brought his eyes down to the two clusters of staghorn sumacs closer to the ranch.

Again, he slowly peered into the darkness, strained his eyes to define shapes, and swore silently as he saw nothing. It had been a slim chance anyway, he murmured, and he started to turn away when he caught sight of some movement at the farthest cluster of trees. He halted, scanned the area again, and suddenly saw the leaves move. He peered harder and managed to discern the figure against the darkness; it finally took shape and became a horse and rider under the trees.

Canyon moved forward, down the slope, and dropped into a deep crouch as he kept to the rear of the two clusters of sumac. The shape grew more defined as he grew closer. He slowed and the man on the horse sat quietly, his eyes on the darkened buildings below, but he wasn't absorbed in intense concentration. He'd be alert to any sound, and Canyon began to inch forward on slow, stealthy steps.

O'Grady reached the rear edge of the trees, paused, then took another careful step as he edged his way under the trees. The still figure made an easy target, but he wanted the man alive and able to answer questions. Canyon crept closer, each step bringing him deeper into the trees. He dropped to one knee as he saw the horse suddenly grow restless. The animal sensed his presence, and he waited as the rider pulled the reins tight to calm the horse. Canyon stayed motionless, hardly breathing, until the horse settled down before he inched forward again.

He had decided against ordering the man to freeze. It allowed for too much of a chance for the wrong reaction. Complete surprise was best, a flying leap to yank him out of the saddle, and only a few feet from his target now, he crept closer. He edged the last foot nearer and halted, close enough now, and he gathered the strength of his powerful thigh and calf muscles. He let his knees bend for a moment and then leapt. He was already into his upward dive, his feet off the ground, when the horse suddenly swung his rump around. Canyon, arms outstretched, felt himself crash into the heavy, muscled rump instead of clamping both arms around his quarry. All he managed was a one-handed grab that grazed the man's arm before he slid off as the horse kicked out.

Canyon cursed aloud in pain as the hoof caught him in the thigh. He flew sideways through the air, drew his arms in, and hit the ground on his side as the horse leapt forward. He flung himself into a roll despite the pain in his thigh, but no shots split the air, no bullets thudded into the ground inches from his rolling form. Instead, he glimpsed the horseman racing away to disappear into the black of the night.

"Damn," Canyon swore as he pushed himself to his feet and winced at the pain in his thigh. Everything had gone awry, wrecked by the turn of a horse's rump. " 'The best-laid plans of mice and men . . .' " he muttered aloud as he began to limp back to where he'd left the palomino. But one thing was obvious: the man was under orders to run rather than fight. Somebody wanted no chance of trails leading back.

Canyon drew a deep sigh and winced when he reached the palomino and pulled himself into the saddle. He rode slowly and felt the lump on his thigh swelling. He left the slope, rode across another low hill, and found a spot to bed down beneath two low-branched hawthorns. He slept on one side on his bedroll, and the night deepened in silence.

When morning came, he dressed gingerly, barely able to pull Levi's over the lump on his thigh. He rode slowly and found a small, deep pond plainly fed by underground springs. He undressed again and sank himself into the cold water. He let out a groan of relief as the cold embraced his thigh. He relaxed, elbows on the ground at the edge of the pond, and let the morning go by as he felt the swelling on his thigh begin to subside. He pulled himself from the pond at noon, lay in the hot sun, and then returned to the water again. By midafternoon, the swelling had gone down considerably from the cool water, and the pain no longer burned. He stayed in the pond long into the afternoon and then let the last rays of the sun dry him off. He dressed, finally able to don trousers with only a few stabs of pain. He made his way to Dry Corn in the dusk and saw Ben Burton waiting outside his office with a sturdy roan.

"I was getting worried about you," the dentist said.

"Had to tend to some natural medicine," Canyon said. "I'll tell you more about it while we ride."

"All right. We've got almost two hours of riding ahead of us," Ben Burton said, and set off at a trot.

Canyon recounted the events of the night before, and when he finished, Ben Burton offered only mild surprise.

"I'd guess somebody from Hal Colbert," Ben said. "It's about time Colbert began to fight back some. Until now he's been just taking it from Roy Gannet. Some folks have been wondering if he has the strength to be a senator."

"You sound as though you're one of them, Ben," Canyon remarked.

"The thought's crossed my mind. I'm voting for him, mind you, but then I know how Washington feels about Roy Gannet and that's more than other folks know," Ben said. "Until I learned that and saw the kind of campaign Gannet's been waging, I had nothing against Roy Gannet. He likes being powerful and he can be overbearing, but I'd never heard of him cheating anybody out of their land or grinding down on the small ranchers.''

''So you think he's still got most of the votes?'' Canyon asked.

''I'm not sure anymore, not with how he's been running his campaign. I'd say it's still damn close.''

''Maybe this Dryad County meeting will give us a sense of things,'' Canyon said, and lapsed into silence as he rode through the night beside Ben Burton.

They kept a steady pace, and when they reached the granary, they found the crowd pretty much inside. The wagons outside belonged to ordinary folks, Canyon noted, pretty much buckboards and one-horse shays. He dismounted and followed Ben Burton inside the long, slant-roofed building.

The crowd had already taken up all the long, flat wood benches at the front of the granary, and he and Ben found a spot to stand along one wall. Canyon's brow creased into a tight furrow as he saw the compact, high-busted figure in the front row. She turned, and her frown of surprise echoed his as she quickly rose and came over.

''More surprises,'' Glenda said.

''Ben Burton asked me to come along. I didn't expect to be seeing you here,'' Canyon answered.

''Hal Colbert is in Ferris County. As he can't be in two places at once, he asked me to speak here for him,'' Glenda explained.

"Now I'm especially glad I came." Canyon smiled.

"Let's talk when the meeting is over," she said, her eyes very round and very full of sincerity.

"Why not?" He nodded and she hurried back to her seat as a man in overalls and a red shirt called the meeting to order.

"The election's coming up soon, and we all know how important it is to all of us and to Missouri. Hal Colbert couldn't come tonight, but Glenda Gannet's going to speak for him," the man said, and Canyon smiled at the use of Glenda's family name.

She rose and started forward when a side door of the granary opened and six men entered. Three positioned themselves against one wall and the other three stayed at the back of the crowd. Canyon's eyes narrowed as he surveyed the lot. Hired guns, he grunted. It was in their cold eyes, the harsh set of their faces, and the polished leather of their holsters. He returned his eyes to Glenda as she began to address the crowd.

She spoke well, using simple sentences to portray Hal Colbert as the man who cared about the small ranchers. Most of what she said echoed the speech he'd heard Hal Colbert give earlier, but she did add a few personal anecdotes and she finished to hearty applause. Following her set speech, she answered a half-dozen questions from the crowd with smooth ease. It was only when the last question came that he saw the moment of strain come into her smile.

"Everybody knows there's bad blood between

you and your pa," a thin man got up and asked. "You sure that's not the real reason you're backing Hal Colbert?"

"That has nothing to do with it at all," she answered. "I'm backing Hal Colbert because he's the best man for the job." Whether the reply satisfied anyone was impossible to know, but there were no more questions and Glenda returned to her seat.

The man in the overalls rose again to face the audience, his eyes searching out the six men who had entered late. "Any of you gents here to talk for Roy Gannet?" he asked.

"We're all here for Roy Gannet," one answered, a tall figure in a black shirt, his long-jawed, angular face hard as a pine board. "But we didn't come to make speeches. We came to tell you to vote for Roy Gannet if you know what's good for you, all of you." Canyon watched the man step forward to slowly scan the audience with the eyes of a pit viper. "You don't elect Roy Gannet and you'll pay for it, one way or another. You can count on that. Now, how many of you are smart enough to vote for Roy Gannet?"

Canyon's brow furrowed as he watched the unhappy glances that ran through the crowd and heard the low rumble of discontent rise from the assembled men and women.

A figure rose at the end of one of the long benches, a thickset man with a beard, his hand on the shoulder of the woman beside him. "You can't come here and threaten us this way. We're not a bunch of sheep," he said.

115

"Who're you, bigmouth?" the black-shirted man rasped.

"Sam Jenkins. I'm not afraid to tell you my name. Truth is, I was thinking of voting for Roy Gannet, but I'm sure as hell not going to now. You can go back and tell him I'm not the only one who won't take to being threatened."

"Maybe you won't be voting at all," the black-haired man snarled.

"I'll be voting, all right, for Hal Colbert," Jenkins said.

"Me too, now," a voice from the crowd called out, and a low murmur of agreement rose from the others.

A slow smile spread across the tall man's pine-board face, and his hand lashed out and closed around the shirt of an elderly man near him. Canyon saw the six-gun appear in his other hand. He pressed the muzzle of the revolver against the man's cheek. "Tell me who you are going to vote for, old man," he said.

"I . . . I don't know. I haven't made up my mind," the elderly man stammered.

"I'd make it up damn fast if I were you," the black shirt said, and pressed the muzzle harder into the man's cheek.

Canyon's hand reached to his holster and silently drew the ivory-gripped Colt out. "Let go of him or you're a dead man," he said quietly but clearly, and the black shirt looked up in surprise to see the Colt pointed at him. Out of the corner of his eye, Canyon saw two of the men at the rear start to draw their guns. "Anybody shoots and you get it, that's for sure," he said.

"You're dead before they get me." He saw the man's eyes stay on the unwavering barrel of the big Colt and then, slowly, the man moved his gun from the elderly man's face. "Put it in your holster, nice and slow," Canyon ordered, and the man obeyed. "Now tell them to put their guns away," Canyon said as he held the Colt aimed at the man's heart.

"You heard him," the black-shirted figure growled, and Canyon saw the others obey.

"Now get out—you last," Canyon said, the Colt still in position as the other five figures shuffled to the side door and left. "Your turn," Canyon said.

"I won't forget this, mister," the man growled.

"That makes two of us," Canyon said, keeping his Colt aimed at the tall figure as the man slid out of the door. Canyon heard the sigh of relief and the murmur of gratitude mingle in the crowd, and the man in the overalls called out to him.

"We're thanking you, mister," the man said. "We've not seen you around before this."

"Just visiting Ben Burton," Canyon said. "The name's O'Grady, Canyon O'Grady."

"You're the man who won the race the other day," Sam Jenkins said, and Canyon nodded.

"I guess the meeting's over. We can all go home and think about what we saw and heard tonight," the overalled man said.

"Amen," someone called out, and the crowd began to rise and drift toward the door.

Canyon found Ben Burton's gaze on him. "You

got a pretty good show tonight,'' the dentist said. ''That's the sort of thing Gannet's been pulling all over.''

''It's terror tactics, intimidation, no question of that,'' Canyon agreed even as something inside jabbed at him. But the feeling had neither shape nor form yet, and he said nothing about it. He was watching Sam Jenkins and his wife start to leave the granary as Ben Burton turned toward the door. ''I'm wondering if Jenkins might need some protection on the way home. He really stood up to them,'' Canyon said to Ben.

It was Glenda's voice at his elbow that cut into his thoughts. ''Come back to my place with me, Canyon,'' she murmured, words spoken so low that only he could hear them, and he turned to see the contriteness in her face. ''I was out of line last night,'' she said. ''Plain jealousy, I guess.''

He felt the surprise slide across his face. ''That's as good an explanation as any,'' he said.

Her hand closed around his arm. ''Come back with me. Please. I'll make up for last night.''

''Now I'd be a fool to turn down such an invitation,'' he said, and a tiny smile edged his lips.

''You would be,'' she said.

''Ben will be riding part of the way back with us,'' Canyon said, and she shrugged happily, linking her arm in his as he started for the door.

Outside, he paused to watch Sam Jenkins and his wife drive off in a buckboard and felt a tiny wince deep inside himself. Glenda's warm hand against his drove the moment away. He was probably being an alarmist, he muttered silently. Besides, if Glenda was in the mood to talk, it was an opportunity he couldn't pass up. He walked Glenda to her horse, then climbed onto the palomino, and with Ben Burton alongside, began to ride back.

"Is it difficult for you to stand by and see your pa doing the kind of thing that took place tonight?" the dentist asked Glenda, and her smile was laced with bitterness.

"It would be if I felt the way I ought to feel about him. But to me he's not my pa, not anymore. He's some stranger I've known all my life," Glenda said.

"Guess it helps to feel that way," Ben said quietly, empathy coloring the few words, and they all fell silent for most of the ride back.

Ben went on toward town as Glenda turned toward her place, and only Canyon caught the nod and half-smile behind Ben's rimless eyeglasses. When they reached her place, Glenda took him inside, turned a lamp on low, and brought out a bottle of good sipping whiskey.

"Don't mind if I do," Canyon said as he took the glass offered him.

"How'd you and Ben Burton get so friendly?" she asked as she sat on the settee beside him.

"Had a tooth bothering me and stopped in to see him," Canyon said. "We got to talking. I guess we just hit it off."

"He doesn't seem like the kind of man you'd find interesting," Glenda commented as she sipped from her glass.

Canyon smiled and shrugged. "I find everybody interesting," he said, and reminded himself again to chose answers with care. Carla was curious about him, but hers was a soft-edged curiosity. Glenda's rose from a sharp, probing mind, and that was always the more dangerous. "Stodger offered me a job," he told her. "He said six of his men just up and left, new hands he'd only just hired. Seeing as how I did in six who tried to burn you down, I'd say that's stretching coincidence."

She thought for a moment. "What else are you saying?"

"That you could be wrong about your father doing it," he said.

"Because it was Stodger's men? He and Daddy are pretty friendly. Daddy could have him do it for him," Glenda said. "Daddy wasn't at that meeting tonight, either, was he? Not personally, but he was behind what happened."

Canyon's lips pursed. She'd made her point with reasoned forcefulness. He couldn't brush it aside, he realized. But he couldn't embrace it wholly either. The vague feelings of uneasiness still pushed at him, and he felt as though he'd been cast adrift on a sea of dark and swirling currents. "Maybe somebody ought to confront your daddy on this? Maybe then he'd stop."

"He'd only deny it. He's never there when his strong-arm men do their thing. He's too clever for that," Glenda said. "But I didn't ask you back to talk about Daddy."

"No?" he asked mildly, and drained the whiskey. "I thought that's what was on your mind."

"Carla's been on my mind. Carla and you the other night."

"You said you knew Carla was too high and mighty to just fall into bed with anyone."

"That mightn't hold for a second time," Glenda said. "And she might have you come visiting again."

"She might," he conceded. "But it might be just that, a visit."

"I'm not taking that chance," Glenda said, and reached out with both arms, encircled his neck, and drew him to her. He felt her mouth on his, wet and eager, her tongue immediately probing, and he felt himself respond. "Yes, oh, God, yes," Glenda murmured as her lips worked feverishly over his, and he glimpsed her hands pulling at her shirt, all but tearing off buttons as she shed her clothes.

He saw very round, very high breasts, full and compact, a large pink circle on each with a large pink nipple. She yanked off her skirt and bloomers, and his eyes took in the firm, slightly barreled chest, a tiny, convex belly, and a surprisingly small nap that narrowed to full-fleshed, firm thighs and calves.

Her hands were pulling at his clothes, and he helped her quickly, finally rising naked before her. He saw her eyes grow wide as she gazed at his already erect and throbbing maleness. He swung her into his arms and she nodded toward the adjoining room as her hands caressed his chest. He stepped into the bedroom, the lamp from the hallway giving enough light for him to see the wide double bed, and he lay down on it with her as his mouth found one high, round breast. He pulled, sucked, ran his tongue around the pink tip, and Glenda cried out in joy. "Yes, yes, oh, more . . . more, mmmmm," she murmured, half-gasped, then cried out again as he caressed the other high, firm mound.

He let his fingers trace a line down the barrel-like rib cage, across the short waist, then pause at the deep indentation in the convex little belly. He moved down farther, across the small nap that surprised him again with its fibrous stiffness, and he pressed down on the large pubic mound that rose up to meet his touch.

"Oh, Canyon, ah . . . aaaah," Glenda breathed, and her firm, compact torso lifted, fell back, lifted again. "Jesus, take me, take me," she breathed, and he slid his hand down farther, letting his fingers move to the dark warm portal. He found her moist, already spilling forth for him in the eagerness of wanting. He touched the soft wetness, gently with a soft caress, and Glenda's scream was a sudden flash of sound, almost harsh yet softened by ecstasy.

He felt her hand suddenly clamping across his wrist, pushing him deeper. "More, more . . . ah, God, more, deep, all the way in . . . oh, Jesus, Jesus," she gasped, and her firm torso writhed. He obeyed, wanting to obey, eager to taste, explore, sink into the fervidness of her wanting. He pushed into her, caressed, and Glenda cried out in pleasure, keeping her hand closed around his wrist, as if she feared he might leave her. "More, Canyon O'Grady," she whispered. "More, more."

He obeyed again, caressing and stroking her. Her hand finally fell away from his wrist as her torso lifted, twisted, came down again, and he felt her hand find him as she screamed, another sudden flash of sound that seemed to explode from her. Glenda's entire body was lifting, thrusting upwards, imploring, the senses shouting through the flesh, and her hand pulled at him, moved him toward her even as he felt the dewy lips quivering at his touch.

He lifted his hips, came over her, and let her hand pull him forward and guide him into her. Glenda's entire body arched backward as his pulsating strength found her. Her scream spiraled, lingered in the air, then found new strength as he slid forward. The firm, compact thighs slapped against his sides as she writhed and twisted and pumped with consuming fury.

"Yes, yes, yes . . . oh, Jesus, yes, yes, oh, God, oh," Glenda cried out, gasping, screaming, moaning as she pulled his face into the high, round breasts, rubbed him against her almost brutal strength. Her devouring fury was its own erotic explosion, far past denying, sweeping him along on a torrent of raw passion, and he felt himself thrusting with increasing harshness as she cried out in delight.

"More, damn, more," Glenda screamed between gasps, and he pushed harder and felt her flesh grasping at him until suddenly he felt his own spiraling explosion as Glenda continued to dig her thighs against him, her body pumping feverishly and her convex little belly jiggling. Her scream, ripped from deep inside her, drowned out his own guttural gasp of pleasure, and she held him to her, smothered his face against one firm, round breast and quivered against him until, with a long, despairing sigh, her arms fell away and her thighs parted, quivered a moment longer, then dropped to his side.

"Good," Glenda murmured, her eyes closed, her brown hair moist at the edge of her temple. "Good . . . so good, mmmmm." He slid from her finally and her legs drew up to press against his crotch, knees dug in between his thighs. Her eyes opened, staring at him, and a small, smug smile curled around her lips. "It was wonderful," she murmured. "You're wonderful."

"And you're a volcano wrapped in flesh," Canyon said.

Her smile stayed. "Volcanoes are worth visiting over and over," she said.

"They are indeed."

She rose onto one elbow, brought one high, round breast onto his chest, and let the pink tip rub gently across his skin. "When are you going to tell me about Canyon O'Grady?" she slid at him.

"I have told you." He laughed. "Young ladies are always looking for some secret. They're never content to see an ordinary man."

"Especially you," she said. "There's nothing ordinary about you. Tinker, wanderer, you say. Well, what made you wander here, Canyon?"

"Fate, maybe," he said. "Maybe I was meant to come here and find you."

"I'd like to believe those romantic words." Glenda smiled and her eyes caressed his body.

"But I'm a realist, not a romantic. No flights of fancy for Glenda Gannet."

"It's Gannet now, is it? What happened to Taylor?" Canyon asked.

"Gannet, Taylor, it's all still me." She shrugged.

"But you do have your own flights of fancy. You insist your father killed your husband, but you've no real proof. You let bitterness send you into flights of anger, and that's no good," he said.

"That's realism, Canyon O'Grady, not fancy," she corrected him firmly. "As real as my making love to you just now. Don't tell me that wasn't real."

"Oh, that was real indeed, lass," he said, and she sat up, the firm, compact breasts bouncing with the sudden movement.

"Go now, Canyon. I've no energy left for any more tonight," she said.

"I'm not surprised at that," he said honestly.

"Even a volcano has to gather itself before its next eruption," Glenda said, laughter in her voice.

"Indeed," he said, and finished dressing. "I'll be by for that."

She walked to the door with him, nakedly beautiful, all her compact vibrancy mirrored in her loveliness.

He paused at the door to look hard at her. "Tell me one thing, no lies in it. How'd you know I was at Carla's the other night? I know somebody's been watching the Gannet place," he said.

"One of Colbert's men," Glenda said. "He told Hal, and Hal told me. You see, I'm not the only one curious about you, Canyon O'Grady."

"You've no need for it, none of you," he said, and she let her lips cling to him for a moment more before he slipped outside and climbed onto the palomino. Her answer fitted and he appreciated her honesty, but he wondered why he felt conquered as he rode into the darkness. He wondered, and was surprised by the pleasantness of the feeling.

He steered his horse to town and took a room at the inn. He wanted to see Ben Burton in the morning and the idea of a soft bed appealed to him.

When he undressed, he lay in the dark of the small room and enjoyed the memories of Glenda that still washed through him. She had been a surprise, a consuming explosion that pushed aside everything that had happened earlier in the evening into a dim corner of his mind. He'd let it stay there till morning, he murmured to himself, and closed his eyes in welcome sleep.

8

He woke with the morning sun, washed, dressed, and breakfasted on a sweet roll and coffee at the inn while he let his thoughts return to the early part of the evening. He went over everything that had been said and done at the granary, and realized that the uneasy feelings he'd had then were still with him. And still undefined, he grunted with a frown as he led the palomino along the street toward Ben Burton's office. He reached it, tied the horse to the hitching post, and saw Ben open the door for him, his plain, mild face tight behind the rimless glasses.

"Trouble?" Canyon asked as Ben closed the door behind him.

"Sam Jenkins and his wife were murdered on their way home last night," Ben said, and Canyon heard the groan that rose from deep inside him.

"Oh, good God, good God," he said, and the pain that turned inside him was real. "My fault, my fault."

"You can't blame yourself for it. You've been after a chance to find out whatever more Glenda might know. The chance came along last night and you took it," the dentist said.

"That's not the real truth of it," Canyon said. "That's what I told myself last night, but truth is that I saw a chance to lie next to a warm body, and I grabbed at it. Two people are dead because of it. I should've gone after Sam Jenkins last night. I knew it and turned away from it."

"They might've gotten to them anyway," Ben said. "Gannet's men killed Sam and Mary Jenkins and sent a message to everyone who was there: fall in line or end up the same way."

Canyon frowned as he listened to Ben. "Something's wrong about it, something's just not right," he said, and drew a questioning frown back. "I haven't been able to give it shape yet, but it's there, something more than we're seeing."

"It seems pretty damn plain to me," Ben said.

"Almost too plain."

"Meaning what?"

"I told you, I can't figure it out yet, but I feel it, something that doesn't fit right. I'll nail it down. Meanwhile, I'm going to throw some dirt in Roy Gannet's face and see what comes back," Canyon said.

Ben Burton nodded and Canyon strode from the office, climbed onto the palomino, and raced out of town. The guilt and anger rode with him as he crossed the low hills to the Gannet ranch. A cowhand was just opening the corral for the old horses when he arrived, and he saw Owen Dunstan standing outside the main house beside the big bay. The man turned his usual disdainful sneer at him as Canyon dismounted.

"Came to see Roy Gannet," Canyon growled.

"He's not here," Dunstan said.

"Then I'll talk to Carla," Canyon said.

"She doesn't want to see you," Dunstan said.

Canyon frowned. "I'll let her tell me that."

"She gave orders. She's not seeing you," Owen Dunstan repeated.

"The hell she's not," Canyon muttered, and started to the house. Dunstan moved to block his path. "I'm not armed," he said. "Throw your gun down and I'll give you a lesson in manners."

Canyon paused, his eyes growing narrow. It was time to dispense with Owen Dunstan and his sneering arrogance. He lifted the Colt from its holster and dropped it into his saddlebag, turned back, and moved toward the man.

Dunstan took a step backward, then two more and was almost against the big bay. Suddenly, with a quick, whirling movement, he reached behind him to the edge of the horse's saddle, and when his arm came down, he held the riding crop in his hand. He swung it at once, a flat arc that Canyon barely managed to pull away from.

"A gentleman, are you?" Canyon growled. "More like a lily-livered coward, I'd say."

Dunstan's answer was another slashing blow with the riding crop, and again Canyon ducked away. Dunstan followed, lashing out with vicious blows, all aimed at ripping his face open, Canyon saw. Any one of the blows could leave a lifelong scar, and Dunstan was quick, his movements darting and dangerous. Canyon dodged another slashing thrust, then tried to come in underneath with a left hook but had to twist away as Dunstan answered with a downward blow that almost caught him. The man's reflexes were quick, Canyon noted grimly, and he tried a feint and saw Dunstan ready to bring the riding crop around instantly.

Canyon feinted again, but Dunstan didn't respond to it and Canyon was forced to duck and twist to avoid two slashing, whistling blows of the riding crop. He moved sideways and tried a left jab. Dunstan brought the crop down at once, but this time Canyon's leg kicked out, a short, stiff motion. His heel connected with Owen Dunstan's shin, and the man swore in pain.

Dunstan bent low for an instant, but it was enough for Canyon's straight left to whistle in over the riding crop. The blow landed on Dunstan's jaw, and he straightened up, quivered, then staggered back while Canyon's next blow caught him on the jaw again. Dunstan staggered back again, the riding crop falling from his hand. Canyon brought up a looping right that lifted the man from his feet and sent him sprawling on the ground. Dunstan lay still, his jaw already beginning to swell, and Canyon stepped over him on his way to the house.

He was about to burst in when the door opened and he faced Carla, her long figure wrapped in a white robe, jet-black hair falling loosely, and black eyes blazing with dark fury. ''And thoroughly beautiful,'' Canyon murmured in honest amazement.

"Get out of here and never come back," Carla hissed.

"What's this all about, lass?" Canyon frowned. "What's digging into you so?"

"Rotter. Bastard. That's all you are under all that fine charm. Well, Glenda's welcome to you," Carla blazed, and Canyon felt the frown dig deeper into his brow.

"Glenda? What's Glenda got to do with this?"

"Oh, she was here first thing this morning, just bursting with the details of how good it was in bed with you," Carla flung out and Canyon felt the shock waves sweep over him. They quickly gave way to silent rage.

"What did you say to her?" Canyon asked.

"Nothing. I wouldn't give her the satisfaction or the chance to learn something against me," Carla said, and Canyon felt grateful for small favors. "I thought you had some honor to you, especially when you were willing to let me out of the wager. I see I was wrong. That was no doubt just cleverness on your part."

"You didn't want to be let out of your wager and you know it. Besides, that was between us."

"Hah," Carla snorted, little dots of red in the whiteness of her cheeks. "I guess that's how you get your pleasure, going from one to the other like a damn bumblebee, laughing all the time, I'm sure."

There was hurt inside her fury. Or was it mere chagrin? He couldn't be sure. "No, it wasn't that way at all," he told her.

"I wouldn't believe anything you said now," Carla flung back. "And you've the nerve to come visiting me this morning, looking innocent as a newborn babe. You're shameless, Canyon O'Grady.''

"I came for other reasons, to see your father," he said.

"He has nothing to say to you," she snapped.

"I'll let him tell me that," Canyon said, turned, and strode from the house. A quick retreat was the best course, he murmured to himself. He knew he wouldn't be able to break through Carla's fury. Not that he could exactly blame her, he grunted, and swore silently at Glenda. When he stepped outside, he saw Roy Gannet riding to a halt. The man stared down at Owen Dunstan, who was just stirring into wakefulness.

"What's going on here?" Gannet boomed out as Canyon approached.

"An interruption," Canyon said. "I was at the Dryad County meeting last night. Two people who stood up to your bully boys were murdered.''

"I heard about it in town," Roy said.

"You have any answers?"

"I didn't send those gunslingers. I don't know anything about it." Roy Gannet frowned.

"You think anybody's going to believe that?"

Gannet's face reddened. "I don't give a damn what anybody believes. I haven't done any of the things they accuse me of doing.''

"Well, now, who could it be going around threatening people to vote for you? Perhaps the ladies' quilting society?" Canyon thrust.

"I can do without the sarcasm, O'Grady," Gannet said, his lips growing thin.

"I think most folks can do without murder and threats."

"Dammit, I can't be held responsible for everyone who goes out on his own to campaign for me."

"You can try," Canyon said quietly.

"Forget him, Father. He's nobody you can trust," Carla's voice interrupted, and Canyon turned to see she had followed him from the house. "Besides, what does all this matter to you, Canyon O'Grady? You're someone just passing through."

Canyon smiled. Jealous fury had turned probing curiosity into active suspicion. "You're right, I am just passing through, but I've an old-fashioned idea that elections ought to be honest and men ought to be free to vote their conscience."

"You're so good with words," Carla sniffed.

"More than words. Or is your memory so short, lass?" He smiled.

"To hell with you, Canyon O'Grady," she blazed, spun on her heel, and half-ran into the house.

"Unless you've more than accusations you can't prove, don't bother setting foot on my land again, O'Grady," Gannet said.

"I'll try to get that proof for you," Canyon said, and climbed onto the palomino. He rode from the house with Roy Gannet's eyes following him.

Canyon frowned as the uneasy feelings inside

him began to gather shape. Roy Gannet's answers continued to bother him. He had expected denials from the man, but he'd also expected more cleverness wrapped around them, something more-thought-out than simple shrugs and putting blame on unknown, overzealous adherents. But he put Roy Gannet aside as he cut across a hillside and turned west. He had another stop to make before returning to Dry Corn and Ben Burton, and the anger was seething inside him when he reached Glenda's place.

She was sweeping off the front porch as he rode up and reined to a halt. Her high, round breasts moved in unison, her firm, compact figure provocatively attractive in tight Levi's and an even tighter gray shirt.

"This is a surprise." She smiled as he dismounted and strode toward her.

"Everybody deserves a surprise. I had mine a little while ago," Canyon snapped, and saw her brow furrow as she entered the house with him.

"What was it?" she asked.

"It was Carla," he said angrily, and she stared back at him. The smile took a moment to touch her lips, but it broadened quickly. "You want to tell me why?" Canyon flung at her.

"Why?" Glenda echoed, the smile becoming almost dreamy. "Because I won for the first time. I had someone first, before she had the chance. I had someone before she did. Carla the beautiful, Carla the glamorous, Carla the favorite, always the first to take whatever she wants. But not this time. It was worth the waiting just to see her face."

"Was that all last night meant to you?" Canyon asked, and cursed at himself for sounding like a wounded maiden with words he'd had thrown at himself often enough. "Was last night just a chance for revenge on Carla?" he asked, rephrasing the question and quickly realizing that it didn't sound any better.

A private wisdom touched Glenda's face. "Last night was a lot of things," she said. "I enjoyed all of it. I thought you did."

His lips thinned and he swore silently again. He had the feeling of being in a place he recognized but with everything changed around, and he was hearing words that were being thrown back at him from out of times past. "Yes, I did, but I didn't need to push it in anyone's face."

"Everyone has their own needs." Glenda shrugged, and suddenly her face hardened. "Why'd you go running to see Carla this morning?" She frowned.

"I didn't. I went to see your father. The rest just happened," Canyon said. "You hear about Sam Jenkins and his wife?"

"Yes," Glenda said. "Is that proof enough for you that he'll stop at nothing? Are you satisfied now that he's a ruthless and cruel man?"

"I'm getting closer to it," Canyon said, unwilling to say more than that.

"Come back tonight, Canyon," Glenda said. "I'll show you that last night wasn't just for Carla's sake. Or do you want me to prove it now?" she asked, and her fingers began to undo the top buttons of the shirt, and the high-coned breasts pressed forward instantly.

"No, I've things that need doing now," he said, and silently applauded his self-discipline as Glenda's smile taunted. He turned away and strode to the door. "None of that excuses you running off to Carla with bedroom tales."

"I won't do it again. I promise," Glenda said, but without the slightest edge of contrition in her voice or in the smugness of her smile.

"I'll be in touch," Canyon said.

He hurried back to the palomino, climbed on the horse, and raced away from the ranch. He slowed only when he was halfway to town, and the noon sun was in the sky when he halted before the dentist's office. He found Burton at the door waiting for him, and the man led the way into his living quarters behind the office.

"You see Roy Gannet?" Ben asked, and Canyon nodded, quickly recounted everything Gannet had said.

"It was weak, all of it," Canyon said when he finished. "I expected a better defense from him."

"Maybe he's just overconfident now. But there might be some good that came out of what happened last night," Ben said. "I've been hearing that people are maybe angrier than they are scared. I hear a lot might vote for Hal Colbert as a way of paying their respect to Sam Jenkins and Mary, and out of plain anger. Gannet might be overplaying his hand."

"That's one of the things that's been nagging at me. It finally took shape this morning," Canyon said. "Gannet may be a lot of things, but he's not stupid. Seems to me a good number of people were going to vote for him anyway."

"True enough," Ben said.

"Then why does he feel he has to send out his bully-boy squads? Why threaten and intimidate and now murder to make his threats stick? He must know he can overplay his hand."

"You answered that yourself when you said that the thirst for power can make a man forget everything else," Ben said, a sadness coming into his plain, drawn face.

"Maybe that is the answer." Canyon shrugged. "But there's more stuck inside me. I just haven't pulled it out yet."

"I've something more important than wondering about things not fitting exactly right," Ben said, reached into the top drawer of a table, and pulled out a flat piece of paper. "This came this morning by stage mail. It's from Washington. They've learned that a courier is due here from a group of very rich slave-state interests with a cash bond to help finance the campaign up here."

"They have any information on when and where?" Canyon asked.

"Indeed they do. The courier is due tonight. The meeting place is the north end of Lake Tebbet, sometime after nine," Ben said. "If we can get to him first and get that bond, we'll have the proof we need against Gannet."

"It would nail down his connection to the slave-state interests," Canyon agreed.

Ben Burton looked down at the piece of paper

in his hands. "Inform our agent at once," he read.

"You've done that now," Canyon said.

Ben put the corner of the paper into the lamp flame and Canyon watched the message quickly become ashes. "I'll go with you," Ben said.

"No, this part's my job."

"I've been in on this from the start. I want to be part of the finish," Ben said, his plain face behind the rimless glasses taking on a kind of pouting righteousness. "It's only fair," he added.

"Maybe it is," Canyon conceded. "All right, we'll meet there. Two riders coming together would surely be spotted. Eight o'clock."

"Eight it is," the dentist said.

"It could be a long night of waiting. You'd best get some sleep this afternoon. I'll do the same," Canyon advised.

"I will," Ben said, and walked the big, flame-haired man to the door.

"If you get there first, get off your horse and stay in the trees," Canyon said. "Don't do anything till I get there, no matter what you see. Understand?"

Ben Burton nodded gravely and Canyon slipped from the office and hurried to climb onto the palomino. He'd just settled into the saddle when he saw Roy Gannet looking at him as he rode by. The man slowed and Canyon let his horse draw alongside him.

"Got a tooth problem?" Gannet asked.

"Had one," Canyon answered.

"Everybody's got problems of one kind or another," Roy Gannet said. "You got that proof you're looking for yet?"

"Soon," Canyon said, and Roy uttered a harsh grunt as he sent his horse into a canter and rode on.

Canyon swore silently. It had been a chance meeting, a moment he wished he could take back, but it had happened and now he could only hope Roy Gannet would not think too much about it. Canyon watched Gannet disappear down the main street of the town, and his lips pulled back in a grimace. Despite everything that had happened, despite everything Glenda had said about her own father, a nagging doubt still prodded at him. A question mark, perhaps small and tattered, still trailed Gannet.

"Canyon O'Grady," the voice called and broke off his musings. He turned to see Glenda in a light pony wagon with maroon upholstery. He slowed and she rolled alongside him with an appraising smile.

"Seems as though everybody's in town today," he commented.

"It's shopping day for me," Glenda said. "I saw you talking to Father."

"I'd not call it that," Canyon said. "A dozen words in all."

Glenda's smile was taunting again. "You coming by tonight?"

"Not tonight."

"You still sulking?"

"No," he snapped more irritatedly than he'd intended.

"Seems to me you are."

"I just have some things that need doing to-night," he said.

"More good deeds?"

"You could say that."

"Who's the lucky girl this time?" Glenda speared, her smile still taunting.

He reined to a halt and his snapping blue eyes had grown hard. "I'll tell you more when I can," he said.

"Just me? Or Carla, too?"

"Who's sulking now?" Canyon returned. "You're a persistent little package, I'll give you that. But I'll say no more now."

"That sounds like a dismissal."

"You can take it that way if you like," Canyon said.

With a smile that had suddenly grown cold, Glenda snapped the reins, and the pony cart rolled forward. He let her disappear from sight before he rode on and halted at the inn. Jealousy, curiosity, rivalry, and possessiveness, they all came together in little Glenda. He'd have to keep her at arm's length until this was over, he decided. He dismounted, tied the horse to the hitching post, and stepped into the inn.

The desk clerk looked up, his wrinkled face creasing into a smile. "You're becoming a regular boarder here, Mr. O'Grady," the man said. "You want the same room back, I take it."

"That'll be fine," Canyon said, and his glance paused at the tall grandfather clock behind the desk. "You've that fine clock there that keeps wonderful time, I'm sure. Could you come knocking on my door at seven-thirty?"

"I could indeed," the elderly man said.

"Much obliged," Canyon returned, and took the key to the room. The request was Canyon's insurance. The clock would add accuracy, and accuracy was important. He wanted to be there before Ben reached the spot.

Inside the room, he pulled off his clothes in the fading light of the afternoon and stretched out on the bed. He hadn't slept much the night before. Glenda had seen to that. And he'd not be sleeping much this night either, he was certain. He lowered the window shade and let himself quickly plunge into the deep, dark arms of slumber.

He slept soundly, the room still, and he was surrounded by darkness when he woke. He sat bolt upright in bed, a furrow creasing his brow as he listened. But he heard only the silence of the little room. There'd been no knock, he realized. He'd snapped awake by himself, his inner senses exploding. But he'd woken up early, the desk clerk was still waiting for the time to come knocking, and Canyon swung long legs over the edge of the bed and dressed leisurely in the darkness. When he finished and his gun belt was strapped on, he opened the door and stepped into the dimly lighted hallway. He strode the few yards to the front desk and halted. The elderly clerk was not in the chair behind the desk and Canyon's eyes went to the big grandfather clock. The curse rose in his throat and froze there. The hands of the old clock pointed to eight.

He leaned across the top of the counter but still didn't see the man, and he started to spin away when he heard the moan. He tracked it to the closed door of a closet behind the desk and was at the door in two long strides. He yanked it open and stared at the small figure inside the broom closet, gagged and bound. He pulled the man up on his feet and tore the gag from his mouth. "What happened?" he barked as he began to undo the clerk's wrist bonds.

"Two fellers, they came in and asked for you," the elderly clerk said, his voice quavering. "I told them you didn't want to be bothered till seven-thirty. Next thing I know they hit me, tied and gagged me, and threw me into the closet."

The man's wrist ropes loosened enough for him to do the rest himself, and Canyon spun and raced from the inn. Outside, he vaulted onto Cormac and sent the horse racing through the darkened town. He let the horse go full out, powerful muscles racing across the hills while he flung curses into the wind.

Roy Gannet had seen him with Ben Burton. Who else had? Had Ben's role as the government's contact man been discovered? Had the courier been preceded by others who knew about it? The questions flew through Canyon's mind. Had they seen him with Ben and decided to play it safe and keep him out of the way? The questions had no answers, but they all added up to one thing: Ben Burton was in real danger. Why, what, or who could wait. The important thing was to reach Ben, and Canyon kept the palomino racing at a gallop.

As he charged down a low hill, he saw the sparkle of moonlight on water and veered to the right as he approached Lake Tebbet. He slowed as he moved into the trees that surrounded the lake, then halted when he'd ridden as close as he dared. He leapt to the ground to run on soft steps. He listened intently as he peered through the trees, and he was almost at the shoreline of the lake when he saw the lone horse standing quietly to one side. The ivory-gripped Colt was in his hand as he crept forward, and then he recognized the animal as Ben's mount. His eyes scanned the edge of the trees again, moved down to the sand near the water's edge, and felt the pit of his stomach tighten as he saw the figure lying facedown, one arm outstretched in the sand.

He raced forward and dropped down on one knee beside Ben, and it was only then that he saw the dark-red stain that was still spreading across the sand. His oath hung silently on his lips as he saw the deep knife slash that ran from one side of Ben's neck to the other.

"Oh, God, oh, good God," Canyon breathed. "Damn their rotten souls." He was still staring down at Ben when he saw movement in the outstretched arm. A spiral of excitement rushed through him. Canyon reached down, lifted Ben's head, and saw the stream of red flow more quickly from the slashed throat. He quickly lowered Ben's head to the ground again.

"Who was it, Ben?" Canyon asked tightly. "Tell me." He leaned closer, saw Burton's lips move, but only a wheezing sound came from them. Ben's plain face twisted in pain as he tried again to form words, but the knife slash had severed his vocal cords.

"Did you see them, Ben?" he asked. "Try once more. Tell me."

Ben Burton's lips only quivered and pulled back in soundless agony, but Canyon saw the outstretched arm move. Burton's index finger uncurled and moved in the sand of the shoreline. With agonizing slowness, the finger began to trace a line in the sand and Canyon watched, his eyes riveted on the emerging pattern. Burton's forefinger traced a round half-circle, slowly rounding out the bottom. He was forming a letter, Canyon realized and he watched the finger start to move up from the bottom of the half-circle, pause, then laboriously form a crossbar.

Ben's finger stopped, fell away, and Canyon heard the final, shuddering sigh come from the prone form. Ben Burton lay still. But in the stained sand, he had traced the letter G.

9

Canyon stared at the uneven, halting line of the letter traced in the sand. Ben Burton had tried to answer in the only way left to him. The sickness still in the pit of his stomach, Canyon rose and with one foot obliterated the letter. A message had been left, and right now he was the only one who knew that. He'd keep it that way, he decided, and he stared again down at the lifeless form of Ben Burton, at the slash that had gone deep through his throat. The uneven tracing in the sand was imprinted in his mind. The one letter G seemed all too clear. Certainly on the face of it, under the circumstances that surrounded it.

The courier had obviously arrived, had been met, and Ben Burton had paid with his life. Canyon dropped to one knee beside the still form, murmured the quiet words of sorrow and prayer, then lifted Ben onto his horse. He laid him facedown across the saddle and began to lead the animal through the trees. When he reached the place where he'd left the palomino, he climbed onto his horse and continued the slow, painful journey to the edge of the trees.

He had just started to move into the open when a volley of shots exploded, and as one grazed past his temple, Canyon flung himself sideways from the saddle. He hit the ground rolling and managed to disappear into the brush at the edge of the treeline while bullets plowed into the ground after him.

The fusillade ended, and he saw the four horsemen appear, charging toward him, spread out, horses at a gallop. A grim smile edged Canyon's lips as he lay in the brush, the ivory-gripped Colt in his hand.

"You think you took me down," he murmured aloud. "I've a surprise for you, lads." Staying low, he raised the revolver, took aim at the horseman to the far right while he measured the gap in between the next rider. His finger tightened on the trigger, and the attacker on the right went down with his first shot. Canyon saw the next rider try to turn his horse, but the Colt had shifted already and Canyon's next shot exploded through the night. The man quivered in the saddle as the reins dropped from his hand. His horse leapt forward and the man flew out of the saddle almost in a backward somersault.

But Canyon's eyes were already on the other two attackers, and he saw that both had reached the trees and jumped from their horses. Canyon stayed low in the brush and heard one of the two moving toward him through the trees. The man approached almost directly until he suddenly grew silent.

Canyon peered through the darkness and strained his ears, caught the faint rustle of the low brush. The man was crawling now, moving toward him. But the other one had gone his own way in silence, probably circling to his left. Canyon cursed under his breath. They would catch him in a cross-fire, and there was little he could do about it. He hunkered down farther, his eyes on the top of the brush directly in front of him and he saw the faint movement of the leaves.

Canyon cursed silently and hoped that luck would be his. Flattening himself on the ground, he waited. The attacker didn't dare show himself. He'd rely on spray-firing a fusillade of bullets and hope that at least one would find its target. The second man would wait, hold his fire in case their target returned fire. It was a classic maneuver, and he could do little but play it out, Canyon grimaced as he stayed flattened.

He counted off seconds, then minutes, as the attacker in front of him took the opportunity to crawl a few feet closer. Suddenly, the night erupted in a furious volley of gunfire. The man was firing with two guns, Canyon realized, and the bullets whistled inches over his head, slammed into the brush on both sides of him, the spray fire dangerously close.

Canyon continued to lay flattened, unmoving, and as suddenly as it had started, the firing ended. The man had emptied both guns and Canyon raised his head at once, brought the Colt up as he peered forward through the brush. The attacker waited a moment before rising, but he finally pushed up over the top of the brush, his guns reloaded. But the red-haired man was ready to grasp that split second's opportunity. The Colt barked, and the man's half-scream vanished as the base of his throat flung a stream of red into the air.

Canyon had already thrown himself sideways as the burst of gunfire came from his left, shots more accurate and in a tighter pattern as the shooter caught the flash from the Colt. Canyon rolled, cursed as he felt the Colt tear from his hand when a shot grazed the barrel. He let the gun fall, twisted his body to land on his side, and lay still. The attacker stopped firing and Canyon heard the footsteps moving out of the brush. Peering through eyes that were closed to tiny slits, he saw the man's boots come into his circle of vision, his legs take shape as he stepped closer.

Canyon lay motionless on his side and saw the man's boot come out, push his stomach to flip him onto his back. Canyon started to turn, his body limp, when his arm shot out, curled around the man's ankle, and yanked. With a curse and a shot that went wild, the man toppled backward and Canyon hurtled up at him, drove a knee into the man's belly, and heard the grunt of pain that followed. He got one arm out, his hand closing around the man's gun hand as he fell half over the figure.

But the attacker had a wiry strength that found a new surge of power in desperation, and Canyon found himself rolled sideways, the man trying to bring the gun into his chest. Canyon fought back, using the strength of his own arm and shoulder muscles to force the gun away from himself. With another roar of desperation and an explosion of strength, the man rolled with him to end up half atop him. Again, despite Canyon's hold on his wrist, his attacker brought the gun down and Canyon saw the barrel turning toward him. Cursing under his breath, he brought his right leg up, twisted his body, and the man went off-balance. Canyon jammed the man's hand downward just as the gun went off, then saw the surprise flash in the man's face. The surprise became openmouthed pain and the man went limp, his eyes rolling back into his head. Canyon released his grip and stepped back.

The man sank to his knees, a line of red beginning at his abdomen and continuing on downward through his groin. Not unlike a giant balloon suddenly deflated, he collapsed on the ground, the gun falling from his hand.

Canyon's eyes were blue agate as he stared down at the man, then walked to where the other one lay. He retrieved his gun, strode to the other two men, and peered down at each. They were all part of the group of six that had interrupted the Dryad County meeting. The other two had probably gone with the courier while these four circled back to lay in wait. But he had slipped through and reached Ben's slain form first. He turned back to the palomino, slowly rode through the night and back to town, where he woke the undertaker.

"My God, it's Ben Burton," the man said as he came out in his long johns. "He didn't have any enemies."

"Sometimes a man lives two lives," Canyon

said. "You see he gets a proper burial. I'll see you get paid for it."

"Sure thing. A lot of folks will turn out for Ben Burton," the undertaker said. "I'll take care of everything."

Canyon gave him the reins of Ben Burton's horse and turned away, his jaw tight. He rode from town while thoughts dark as the night tumbled through his mind. He found a low-branched bitternut, spread his bedroll, and stretched out on it. When he finally fell asleep, the whirling thoughts still filled his mind, and they were still there, instantly leaping up for attention like so many unruly children, when he woke with the morning sun.

He slowly washed and dressed as he let his mind go over everything that had happened since he arrived in Missouri. He turned every detail with deliberate slowness and finally ended at the murderous events. The letter traced in the sand burned inside his mind with the same dark, throbbing fire it had when he first stared down at it. He let a good part of the morning go by as he examined every painstaking detail. He had to be sure. Or at least reasonably sure. Time was running out, and so was his ability to move around freely. He had been connected to Ben Burton last night, though he was certain they didn't know how. Yet the connection would suffice. He'd have to move more carefully now.

The cash bond was probably already providing more ammunition to win the election with, he muttered grimly as he climbed onto the magnificent horse and rode slowly down the hillside.

Plans took shape inside his mind as he rode. He wandered through the countryside, his gaze scouring the land as he paused frequently and then rode on. He sought a particular place, one that could be found without difficulty and held the natural elements he needed.

The morning grew hot as it neared noon, but he finally found the spot that conformed to all the things he sought: a small arbor, a tiny clearing in the center of it, and thick brush and tree cover on all sides. It was only a few dozen yards from a tall, three-spired rock formation that had to be known by everyone who lived in the region. That much was done, he nodded in satisfaction and patted the palomino's smooth, powerful neck.

"Time to move on," he murmured. "When you can't get the wolf, you bring the wolf out to you."

He rode forward, easing the horse into a trot, but now his eyes swept the terrain as he rode. He knew he could no longer afford the luxury of riding casually through these low hills. But, finally satisfied that no one followed or watched him, he relaxed some and was moving toward the Gannet place when he saw the horse and rider going up into the hills to his right. He watched the long jet-black hair glisten in the sunlight as it hung down beneath her shoulders. Carla's slender, supple body swayed gracefully with the horse's movements. She wore Levi's and a pale-green shirt, and he noted a small leather sack hanging from the saddle horn.

He turned the palomino, cut across the hillside, and moved into a stand of black walnut to draw parallel with her as she stayed in relatively open land. The furrow traveled across his brow as he watched her turn into a narrow passage between two tall rocks. He spurred the palomino up onto higher land to see her emerge from the passage, rein her horse into a sharp right, and go down another narrow pass.

Canyon reined to a halt as Carla disappeared from sight. He waited a few moments longer and then sent the palomino down to the narrow passages below. He followed in her footsteps, moving carefully, and suddenly reined up as the passage opened and he saw a small, crystal-clear spring-fed pond tucked in the center of a circle of boulders. He saw the white flash of Carla's shoulders as they disappeared into the water, and he watched her ebony hair float atop the crystal-blue pond, a black lily pad. Carla swam back and forth across the small pond, diving below the surface, coming up in a flash of long white arms, graceful and fluid as an otter at play.

Canyon sent the palomino forward, emerged from the narrow passage, and halted near the edge of the pond. Carla whirled in the water as she saw him dismount.

"What are you doing here?" she asked, treading water and letting only her head and shoulders show.

"Saw you riding. I followed," he said diffidently.

"You've added oggling to your other sterling characteristics?" she asked tartly, and moved closer to the shoreline.

"Not at all. I've always considered oggling to be a perfectly proper pastime," Canyon said. "Did you hear about Ben Burton?"

"Yes, one of our hands came from town with the news. You brought him in, I hear," Carla said. "How did you happen to find him?"

"Just riding by," Canyon said.

"I'm not swallowing that. What are you doing here, Canyon O'Grady? You suddenly turn up, and in no time you're full of questions and in the thick of things." Carla frowned.

"I've a talent for being at the right place at the right time. Or is your memory so short?"

She stared back at him with cool appraisal and ignored his barb. "It seems to me that you're like a bad penny, always turning up at unexpected places," Carla remarked. "Though I suppose some of them are not really unexpected."

"Such as?"

"Any convenient bedroom," Carla snapped.

He let his lips purse and decided to try another approach. "You keep saying Glenda lies. You ever think maybe she lied about that?"

Carla let a slow, chiding smile touch her lovely, fine-edged lips. "She does lie. And she's sick, twisted up inside. But she wasn't lying about that. A woman can always tell when another woman is telling the truth about those moments."

Canyon shrugged. "Sometimes there's a good reason why a thing happens," he said, falling back on a note of mystery.

"Any chance you can get is a good reason to you," Carla flung back.

"Harsh words again," Canyon said. "And unjust."

"Harsh, perhaps, but not unjust."

"Answer a few questions for me and I'll go away and let you get out of there," Canyon said. "Where were you last night?"

"At home."

"Your pa?"

"I don't know," she said. "I didn't see him after I went to my room."

"Then he could've left the house," Canyon said.

"He could've been there, too. It's a big place. I often don't see him even though he's there," she said. "And I'm not answering any more of your questions."

Canyon felt the surprise stab at him as she rose in the water and stepped onto the land. He stared at her beauty as she stepped toward him. Her slender body glistened with droplets of water, her breasts swaying gently as she walked, the black triangle an ebony spot against her alabaster skin. A tiny droplet of water hung from the very tip of one fiery pink nipple and finally shook itself loose as she walked toward him. She halted, turned, let herself stretch, and he saw her smile at the hungering admiration in his eyes. She was parading her beauty for him, flaunting all her desirable loveliness, and he felt the stab of anger inside himself.

"Why?" he growled.

"A reminder. Letting you see what you gave up for little Glenda."

"She doesn't have your kind of beauty."

"Well, you're stuck with whatever it is," Carla said with sudden harshness, then turned and strode to her horse. She pulled the little leather sack open and pulled a towel out of it. She faced him as she dried herself, her smile smug and taunting.

"What makes you think I won't just go and take you right here and now?" Canyon frowned.

She met his glowering eyes with cool confidence. "Other men maybe. Not you."

"What makes you so sure?"

"You wouldn't give me that satisfaction," Carla said.

He let a grim laugh escape his lips. The wisdom of a woman, he murmured inwardly. All the more powerful because it came from beyond reason and logic. He watched her dry herself and dress with deliberate slowness, and he climbed onto the palomino when she went to her horse.

"I'll see you home," Canyon said.

"Anger and desire reduced to politeness." Carla laughed, and he swore silently at her.

"No, I want to speak to your father," he snapped, and followed her through the narrow passages.

Once out of the hills, he rode beside her, and though she rode in haughty silence, he could feel the smugness of her. They reached her place and he saw Roy Gannet come from the main house as they rode to a halt and Carla dismounted.

"What are you doing riding with him?" Gannet boomed at his daughter.

"He said he was coming to see you," Carla answered, and strode on into the house. She paused at the door and glanced back, her smile fashioned of small victory.

"I've nothing to say to you, O'Grady," Roy Gannet said.

"I might have that proof for you," Canyon said, and saw the man's frown grow deeper.

"Proof that I hired those gunslingers? That they killed Sam Jenkins on my orders?" Gannet frowned. "You won't get any proof on that because there isn't any."

"So you keep saying," Canyon answered. "You know that big boulder with the three peaks due north of here?"

"I know it." The man nodded.

"There's a small black oak arbor a dozen yards west of it," Canyon said. "I'll be there at nine tonight. I'll have that proof."

"Why there?" Roy questioned.

"I'm not coming here with it," Canyon said. "I'm not that big a fool."

"And I'm going out to meet you for something that doesn't exist," Roy Gannet threw back. "Now, get off my land."

Canyon shrugged as he turned the palomino and slowly rode away. He hadn't expected Roy Gannet to admit interest, but the man had been caustically scornful. Canyon grunted with grim satisfaction. He'd had to put all the pieces into place. He couldn't trust anything to chance.

The day had moved into the afternoon as he turned the horse toward Glenda's place. He rode down to the modest spread and saw Glenda open the door as he reined to a halt and swung to the ground.

"Didn't expect you at this hour," she said. "Does this mean you've stopped sulking?"

"Never was sulking, dammit," Canyon snapped as he followed her into the house and she turned to face him, high, round breasts pressing hard against a tight blouse with a square neck. Beauty wears many faces, he murmured silently as he thought of Carla's little exhibition and caustic remarks. It was a truth too many women refused to admit, because beauty was power, personal, individual power.

"You come to stay the night?" Glenda asked.

"No, I came to tell you that the bait's in the water," he said, and drew an instant frown. "I told your father I had proof of who ordered Sam Jenkins' murder."

"Do you?" Glenda asked.

"Not completely. I told him where to meet me?"

"Where?"

"At a little arbor a dozen yards west of that boulder with the three peaks," Canyon said. "I'm sure you know it," he added, and she nodded. "I'm going to get him to make a mistake that will give me the proof I need. Him showing up might be proof enough."

Glenda stepped to him, her hands coming to press against his chest, concern in her eyes. "You're the bait in the water," she said, and he nodded. "You can't do this. It's too dangerous."

"It's the only way. Time's running out," Canyon said.

"No, find another way," she said, arms encircling his neck.

"There is none," he answered.

"What if he doesn't show?"

"That'd make me take another hard look at everything. It could mean I've been barking up the wrong tree, though it's hard to believe that."

"It could also mean he's even more clever than you thought," Glenda said.

"Yes, it could," he agreed. "But I've got to find out."

"I'm afraid, Canyon. Don't do this. You'll find some other way," Glenda said. "Stay here with me tonight. It's not your fight anyway. You've done enough."

He shrugged and his eyes refused her words. She lifted her arms and the blouse came up, flew over her head, and she faced him bare-breasted, the high, cone mounds jiggling. He reached out and yanked her to him, almost roughly, his hands holding against the soft skin of her back.

"Temptress," he said. "Maybe later. I'll be going now."

She pulled away, annoyance as well as disappointment in her face. "You don't want to listen. Go on, then. It's plain I can't make you stay."

He half-shrugged and turned away. It wasn't a time for words, and he left with her eyes burning into his back. Outside, as darkness began to descend, he rode the palomino north, staying in tree cover for most of the time.

The night was deep when he reached the boulder with the three peaks, and he halted in its shadow and let an almost full moon rise before he moved on again. He made his way into the arbor and the small circle in the center of it. He positioned the palomino in the circle where the horse could be seen from any approach. Canyon moved into the brush to one side of the horse and sank down on one knee and fell silent, drawing only short, soundless breaths.

Time ticked away with agonizing slowness as he waited motionless, only his eyes moving as he scanned the trees and brush around the small clearing from right to left and back again, then started over again at once. The moonlight filtered down into the small circle that was surprisingly bright, and Canyon's lips were a tight line as time continued to drag along.

But suddenly he felt the tightness grip his muscles as he saw the brush move. Someone approached, on foot, slowly. He saw and watched the brush grow still as the figure halted. His hand rested on the butt of the Colt at his side, and the brush moved again, the figure drawing close to the small clearing. Canyon's eyes were narrow, his mouth a grim line as the figure halted again—at the edge of the circle now, obviously spotting the palomino.

Canyon's voice was firm but quiet as he called out. "Come out, Glenda," he said, his eyes on the brush.

The figure took a moment to step into the circle, her hands in the deep pockets of a loose skirt under a gray shirt, an almost sheepish smile touching her lips. Canyon rose and stepped into the clearing and her eyes found him at once. "I had to come. I couldn't let you do this alone," Glenda said, and started to rush toward him.

"No more, Glenda. It's over. No more

games,'' Canyon said, his tone savage, and she halted, frowned at him. ''I know why you're here,'' he bit out. ''Take the knife out of your pocket.''

Glenda stared at him, let bewilderment come into her face. ''What are you talking about, Canyon?''

''The knife, dammit,'' he exploded. ''Take it out of your pocket. Now.''

Glenda continued to stare at him and her eyes slowly grew narrow. A cold smile crossed her face and she slowly pulled her hand from the right pocket of the skirt, her fingers closed around the handle of a hunting knife with a ten-inch blade.

''Throw it into the bushes,'' Canyon ordered, his hand tightening around the butt of the Colt.

Glenda shrugged and obeyed and Canyon watched the knife disappear into the brush. The cold smile stayed on Glenda's lips as she brought her eyes back to him.

''How did you know?'' she asked.

''Little things first, then something not so little,'' he answered.

''Such as?'' she asked with calm curiosity.

''First, your father was holding his own with the voters. He maybe even had an edge. He didn't need strong-arm methods. He had to see it was backfiring, that he was pushing people into voting for Colbert out of anger,'' Canyon said. ''Why did he keep doing it? Ben Burton thought it was just blindness, the thirst for power affecting his judgment. It might have been. I wasn't sure. But that was one of the big things that kept sticking into me until I realized he wasn't doing it. Hal Colbert was doing it all in your father's name. It was damn clever, a kind of double reverse that fooled everybody.''

Glenda's icy smile stayed. "What else?"

"The stable of old horses at your father's ranch. That was one of the little things that kept getting bigger. You see, people don't put aside a basic part of their character. They can't. It's too much a part of them. No man who loved his old and faithful horses that deeply, no man who cared about animals that much, could burn down a stable of horses. It'd be impossible for him." Glenda's cold smile began to vanish as she stared at Canyon with narrowed eyes. "You hired that crew to set fire to your place. They were supposed to do their job and get out, and you'd arrive in time to let your stock out. You'd have saved your stock, but you'd have been able to see that your father was blamed. Only I came along and ruined the whole plan. Your place didn't burn down, so you couldn't accuse him of doing it. Saying he tried was too weak for the proper effect.''

"My, you have been doing a lot of supposing, haven't you?" Glenda said.

"No supposing, my girl. It's all true. It took me a while to put it all together, but I finally did. Poor Ben's murder gave me the last of it," Canyon said, paused, and frowned in thought for a moment. "I thought the wrong thing at first. I misread what Ben had tried to tell me.''

"He told you something?" Glenda shot back scornfully.

"Hard for you to believe, isn't it?" Canyon said. "But that tone is an admission of itself." Glenda's eyes grew dark with fury. "Ben traced a letter in the sand with his last ounce of strength. G, he wrote. I thought it stood for Garret at first. But it didn't. The G stood for Glenda."

"You don't know that. That's more supposing," she snapped.

"Poor Ben's throat was cut from ear to ear. Someone had to get close to him to do that," Canyon said, his voice turning harsh. "He wouldn't have let your father get close to him. None of those hired guns, either. He'd have run, and they would have shot him." Canyon stepped forward, two long strides that brought him to Glenda, and his eyes were blue ice, his jaw throbbing. "It had to have been someone he knew and wasn't afraid of, someone he let come up to him. That was you. G for Glenda."

He saw the cold fury blaze in Glenda's eyes. "Bastard," she hissed.

"You were going to do the same thing to me just now," Canyon rasped. "Rush up to me and cut my throat." His hand shot out, a resounding slap that was hard enough to send her to the ground. "Murderess," he hissed. "Sick, twisted-up little bitch."

A booming voice cut into his fury. "Drop the gun, O'Grady," it said from the brush to his right. "Don't be stupid. You're covered."

Canyon uttered a harsh sound. "Colbert," he bit out, recognizing the voice after a moment. Cursing under his breath, he let the Colt drop to the ground and saw Hal Colbert step out of the trees.

"It took you long enough to get here," Glenda complained as she pushed to her feet. She strode to Canyon, her face almost into his. "Fool," she bit out. "It was so good that night. It could have gone on that way. All you had to do was mind your own damn business."

Canyon's quick smile was rueful. "That's always been a problem with me."

"It won't be any longer," Glenda said.

10

"No," Glenda said to Colbert. "We don't kill him here. Someone might find him. I don't want any more unexplained killings until after the election."

"You're probably right there," Hal Colbert said. "We only have to keep him alive another two days. We'll take him to the cabin."

Glenda nodded. "Tie his hands and put him on his horse," she said, and picked up the Colt, holding it on Canyon while Colbert used a length of lariat to tie his wrists behind him. "Besides, I want to find out more about him. I still don't think he just happened by," she said.

Canyon, with Colbert's help, climbed into the saddle and was led from the arbor to where Glenda's horse waited. They rode with Canyon between them, across the hill and down into a dip in the land that was all but covered by a thick growth of black walnut.

A cabin appeared at the far end of the forested valley, and Canyon saw five men, two he recognized at once as the last of those who had appeared at the Dryad County meeting. One of the men pulled Canyon from the palomino and pushed him into the cabin.

"I'll be right in," Glenda called, and Canyon found himself in a one-room cabin with three cots in it. A table with some plates and eating utensils took up one corner of the room, and he saw a sharply honed, long-handled ax standing in another corner.

Glenda came in with Canyon's saddlebag, which she flung onto the table. She walked over to him and allowed a small smile as she searched him, emptying his pockets, patting his body. "Tie him into a chair," she said, and Hal Colbert directed one of the men as Canyon was strapped into a straight-backed chair, his arms pulled back and rope wound around his chest, his arms, and the chair.

"How did you two fine folks first hook up?" Canyon asked Glenda and Colbert as he sat facing them in the chair. The others had gone outside.

"We first met when Glenda was on a trip into the southern part of the state," Colbert said. "We realized we had a number of interests in common."

"Certain forces were backing Hal to run for senator in the north against Daddy," Glenda said.

"Slave-state forces?" Canyon asked.

"That's right," she answered. "I wanted the same thing they did, to see Daddy defeated, so we decided to join forces." She paused to empty the contents of his saddlebag on the table and began to search through everything as she talked.

"We knew it wouldn't be done just by campaign speeches, so we came up with our plan. The forces backing Hal had information put out in the right circles that Daddy was secretly pro-slave state." She chuckled and Canyon grimaced silently. He wanted to keep her talking, divert her attention from her search of his things, but he saw her pause and hold up the small square of paper that had been at the very bottom of his saddlebag.

Glenda's eyes turned to him, a furrow crossing her brow, and Canyon cursed silently as he saw Colbert step over to her. "Well, would you look at this," Glenda said. "The tinker is something more than a wanderer just passing through, his only purpose to do good deeds." She paused and her eyes went to Canyon as she held the square of paper up. "Canyon O'Grady, Federal Agent," she read aloud, and Canyon saw surprise and anger darken Hal Colbert's face. Glenda put the small square of paper back on the table. "Now, that explains a lot," she said. "We ought to feel complimented, Washington sending a federal agent all the way up here to spy on us."

"The truth is that Washington sent me to keep tabs on your father," Canyon said. "The information your people put out had them convinced he was allied with the slave-state forces. I was supposed to make sure you got a fair chance to win the election. How's that for a laugh?" he finished with grim bitterness.

"Then you can die knowing you did your job," Hal Colbert said, and Canyon swore at the ironic truth in the man's words.

Glenda's voice interrupted and Canyon saw her face had grown tight. "I don't like this," she said. "This puts an entirely different light on things."

"How?" Colbert questioned.

"They sent him. Maybe they sent others. Maybe they're here already or maybe they're on their way," Glenda said. "When they can't contact him, they'll start nosing around more. God knows what they might stir up. I don't want to risk anything going wrong at this late hour."

"What can we do?" Colbert asked.

"Make sure you can't lose. Make sure you're the only candidate," Glenda said.

"Kill your father?" Colbert frowned.

"No, that'd cause questions for sure. We'll make it so that he'll withdraw from the election. With only two days left, there'll be no time to run somebody else against you. The beautiful thing about this is that it'll keep anyone else they've sent here happy. As our friend Canyon O'Grady has just told us, they want to see you win. If Father withdraws, they won't raise the slightest objection."

Canyon swore inwardly as he realized the absolute accuracy of her thinking, even though her fears about other federal agents were unfounded.

"How do we make him withdraw?" Hal Colbert asked.

"Take Carla," Glenda said. "When you have Carla, he'll do whatever you tell him to do. She's the apple of his eye. He'll withdraw. You can be sure of it."

"No," Canyon blurted out. "There's no need

for any of that. I'm the only agent they sent, and the only one they're going to send."

She cast a disdainful glance at him as she spoke to Colbert. "How many men can you get together?" she asked.

"Those here and two more. With me that makes six," he answered.

"That ought to be enough. Take her and bring her back here. Remember, don't hurt Father. He has to be able to make his withdrawal. Just tell him he'll be hearing from you," Glenda said. "He'll obey. He won't do anything to risk Carla's life. O'Grady will be quite safe here with me."

Colbert nodded and strode from the room, and Canyon saw Glenda's eyes on him, her face wreathed in a satisfied smile. She turned away and began to put his things back into the saddlebag.

"Everything neat, eh?" Canyon said.

"Everything." Glenda smiled broadly. "I hate clutter." She dropped the saddlebag on the floor under the table, and Canyon's eyes darted around the cabin. She had put his Colt on a shelf over the table, and he strained his muscles against the ropes and quickly realized he'd never break free. He could use his feet freely enough to move himself and the chair, he realized, and if he could get to the long-handled ax, he might be able to maneuver himself into a position to cut the ropes. He tested the possibility by shuffling his feet forward, and the chair came with him.

Glenda spun around at once, her eyes blazing.

"Try moving again and I'll smash a pot over your head," she hissed.

"I had a cramp in my calf," he muttered.

"Don't get another one," she said, the hate suddenly plain in her eyes. But her threat hadn't been an idle one, he knew, yet he had to get free. This was the only chance he'd have for it. But it was hardly a chance, he realized bitterly. Glenda would keep watch on him from a safe distance, even though his arms were tightly bound to the chair. Yet, if he got her close to him, he might have a chance. He could stand with the chair strapped to him, use his head as a weapon, use all of himself and the chair. But only if he could get her close enough . . .

"I want some water," he said.

"When the others get back," she answered flatly, and sank into another chair beside the table. "Don't try being clever, Canyon."

"I'm not. I'm thirsty," he said, and swore silently. She was unmoved, entirely confident and smugly triumphant. But there was an edge to her, he saw, an inner tension that could easily erupt. If he pressed the right button, he muttered to himself. He'd see if he could draw her out, poke and pry and perhaps hit on something. He'd nothing else left to do, he reminded himself. "Got it all where you want it, don't you?" he said, and Glenda turned a cool stare at him.

"I'd say so," she replied.

"This is all really because you hate your father," he said.

"That's my business," Glenda snapped.

"You're all twisted up, Glenda," Canyon

tried. "Your hate has made it so you can't see anything clearly about your father. You can't see anything clearly about yourself."

"I see very clearly," Glenda said. "And I've a very good memory."

"A memory for hating," Canyon grunted. "That's not memory. That's distortion."

He saw her eyes flash as she peered at him. "You don't know anything about it," she snapped. "I've waited a long time to get back at him, to win my way."

"And at Carla, too?" Canyon speared.

"Yes, Carla, too, Miss Beautiful, Miss Favorite One. Only she has already learned what it's like to be second in line," Glenda said, her voice rising, and Canyon felt the excitement spiral inside him.

"Only you didn't win with Carla," he said, and saw her halt, stare at him.

"What's that mean?" She frowned.

"You lost. That little show you put on for her was a waste of time. She was laughing at you for it," he thrust, and Glenda leapt to her feet, her face darkening.

"What are you trying to say?"

"I'm saying I laid the lovely Miss Carla first," he flung back with a laugh, and saw her lips quiver.

"That's a damn lie. You never did. She never did," Glenda half-shouted.

"Oh, but I did and she did." Canyon laughed again. "That night I spent with her. She wagered I wouldn't win the race. She wagered a night in bed on it."

"Liar," Glenda shouted, and her face was flushed, her hands clenching and unclenching as she took another step toward him. He had found the right button, but he had to be ready, prod her on just a little more. She was close to exploding in an unthinking fury.

"No lie," he said. "You want a description? Breasts a little long but beautifully shaped at the bottoms, that alabaster skin even more so on her bottom and her belly, little nipples of fiery pink, a thick triangle as black as the hair on her head."

"Bastard. Stinking bastard," Glenda exploded, her face distorted in rage as she charged at him, arms outstretched. He bent his face down as far as he could but felt her nails rake the side of his temple. "I'll kill you, you bastard," she screamed, and he felt her hands try to find his throat as she brought her knee up to sink it into his groin. Her face was directly over him when he snapped his head up and smashed the top of his skull against her jaw. She gasped and he saw her stagger backward for a moment. Using all the power of his calf muscles, he flung himself forward with the chair strapped onto his back, drove his head into Glenda's midsection, and heard the breath fly from her. He fell forward with her, landed alongside her as she hit the floor on her back. The chair was an awkward burden, but he managed to turn, saw Glenda gasping for air as she tried to turn on her side, pain in her face and one hand clutched to her abdomen. But she was still conscious, rage still giving her strength.

Canyon rose on one knee, caught his balance

as the chair pulled on him. Again he brought his head around and crashed his skull into Glenda's jaw. This time she toppled on her side and lay still, her breath a wheezing sound. He gathered himself again, pushed to his feet, and walked, bent over, to the ax standing in the corner. He slid down to the floor, lay on one side, and maneuvered himself and the chair until he had his wrist bonds against the blade of the ax. He began to rub the ropes back and forth across the blade and cursed at the slow, cramped pace as he had to halt a half-dozen times to let his arms rest. But the tiny shredded bits of rope that dropped onto his hands were silent words of encouragement, and he cried out in glee when the rope suddenly gave way.

He pulled and wriggled, and the rest of the rope loosened. He tore himself free of the chair and rose to his feet. Glenda was still unconscious, and he debated about trussing her up, but decided not to risk the time. He had been long enough finding a way to reach her, and a lot longer freeing himself from the ropes. Colbert and his men were probably on their way back already, he estimated as he took the Colt from the shelf and slid it into its holster.

He decided not to try to ride out to meet them. There was too much of a chance that he might miss them in the darkness that still cloaked the land. He strode from the cabin, leaving the door partly ajar, then paused outside.

In the distance, the first pink-gray light of dawn touched the tops of the hills, and Canyon scanned the terrain surrounding the cabin. He saw the narrow path on which Colbert and the others would ride to the cabin. He left the palomino hitched to a post. Colbert would be nervous, his senses at heightened awareness. He might readily note the horse missing.

Canyon surveyed the forest land that led to the cabin, and he finally turned and made his way to a hillock densely overgrown with short-trunked hawthorns. He settled down to wait, certain it would not be a long one.

He was right, as he'd hardly settled down when he heard the horses moving along the low stretch of land. He drew the Colt. The dawn had begun to spread, and a faint gray light now filtered over the land. A mixed blessing, he grimaced. It would let him see his targets, but it would also make it almost impossible for him to hide or reach the palomino. But he'd still have those few precious minutes of surprise, he told himself. He'd have to make the most of them.

The sound of the horses grew near and the dawn light stronger. Canyon slid down beside a tree trunk, the Colt already raised to fire. The riders appeared on the narrow path, headed toward the cabin at a slow trot, and he saw Carla on a horse with Colbert. She wore a blue robe over a silk nightgown. They obviously hadn't given her time to dress. They were riding in pairs, he noted, two men in front, Colbert and Carla alongside another horse in the center, and two more riders behind.

Canyon's eyes narrowed, his lips drawn back as he wrestled with the question of whom to take down first. He favored Colbert and the horseman next to him, but Carla was too close to them. He'd wait till they halted and dismounted, he decided as he watched the band of riders rein to a halt outside the cabin. They were just about to dismount when a figure half-fell, half-ran out of the cabin, screaming hoarsely.

"He got away. The bastard got away," Glenda shouted, and Canyon saw the trickle of blood that ran from the corner of her mouth.

"Damn," Canyon swore aloud as he swung the Colt to the first two men. He fired, two shots so quick that the sound of them blended into one, and he saw the two men fall from their horses, one toppling to the left, the other to the right. He swung the Colt, started to tighten his finger on the trigger, and held back as he saw Colbert had brought his horse around to face the hawthorns and Carla was now a shield held in front of him.

"You shoot and you get her," Colbert called out.

Canyon made no reply as he stayed low by the tree and saw Colbert backing his horse away, still using Carla as a shield. He continued backing his horse toward the trees while the other three men, guns in hand, peered toward him. Colbert had backed his horse into the treeline when he shouted a command. "Fire," he said, and the other three men unleashed a barrage of fire that forced Canyon to drop, roll, and fling himself behind a tree to avoid the hail of bullets.

The shooting stopped and Canyon came up to see the three horsemen racing into the trees. Colbert had already disappeared with Carla.

O'Grady rose and streaked for the palomino, and he saw Glenda racing into the cabin. He vaulted onto the palomino, wheeled the horse in a tight circle, and raced for the trees after Colbert and the others. He ducked, an automatic reaction, as the shot exploded and thudded into a tree far off to the side. He flung a glance back and saw Glenda in the doorway, a rifle in her hands as he raced into the trees.

Dawn had come in fully, the first rays of sun streaking down through the trees. The fleeing riders left a wide path of broken twigs and bruised leaves as they raced away, and Canyon closed ground quickly. He finally saw two appear ahead, and he reached down and drew the big Henry from its saddle case. He raised the rifle to his shoulder and fired a fraction of a second after the two men had heard him and turned to look back. They swerved, and his shot missed as both dived from their horses, one to the trees at the right, the other to the left. Canyon yanked back on the reins, and the palomino skidded to a halt. He had already flung himself from the saddle, though, as the shots flew at him from both sides. He'd been a split second from being caught in the middle.

Still holding the rifle, he rose, dodged through the trees, and glimpsed one of the men running, trying to reach his horse where the mount had stopped. The man turned, fired wildly, and Canyon halted, took aim, and fired. The man had almost reached his horse when he went down, one arm flung up in a last, vain gesture.

Canyon went into a crouch and saw the second

man racing through the trees. The man was close enough to his horse to reach it from the other side, and Canyon rose and ran back to the palomino. He leapt into the saddle and sent the horse racing forward as he saw the man in front of him trying to get every ounce of speed from his mount. Canyon closed the short distance quickly, riding low in the saddle, and again the man turned to see him. Panic in his face, the man tried to yank his horse sharply to the right to cut into the deeper part of the forest.

Canyon winced as he saw the man refuse to give the horse a proper chance to slow enough to execute the sharp turn. The horse managed to avoid crashing head-on into a tree, but it scraped along the trunk at almost full speed and Canyon heard the man's scream of pain as his leg smashed into the tree trunk with the full weight of the horse against it. The horse veered away as the man toppled to the ground, and Canyon slowed to see the figure writhing, the left leg torn, already reddened with blood. He sent the palomino racing onward and chastised himself for not being able to summon a dollop of sympathy.

The forest spread out before him and he saw where the last two riders had turned to the left along a place where the trees were less thick. He followed, let the palomino go full out, and frowned as he rode. The sound of his quarry's hooves should have reached him by now, and he quickly pulled the palomino back, slowing from the furious gallop to a canter. He strained his ears and heard nothing except the chatter of morning birds. He slowed again.

The trees thickened suddenly, but his gaze on the ground, he spotted the hoofprints where the two horses had gone to the right. He followed. The terrain suddenly led upward, then leveled off, and Canyon reined to a halt. A dozen yards ahead through the trees, he saw the fallen tree trunk that blocked the way. Carla lay on one side of it, a piece of lariat wrapped around her neck. Behind her, partly hidden on the other side of the tree trunk, Colbert lay with his gun against the back of her neck.

Canyon slid from the palomino and hurried closer on foot. A dense pattern of foliage all but surrounded the fallen tree trunk, but he could see that Colbert was alone with Carla. The man had decided that running further was too dangerous, and Canyon realized that he'd chosen the spot to set a trap, using Carla as both bait and hostage.

Canyon allowed a grim smile as he edged closer and again came to a halt. The trees and thick foliage formed a green curtain around the fallen tree, and Canyon brought his eyes back to Carla. He saw fear and anger mixed in her face. The robe had come open, the silk nightgown beneath it twisted to reveal the beautiful alabaster mound of one breast.

Canyon moved forward and purposely let a twig snap.

Colbert's reaction was instant. "Come on, O'Grady. I know you're out there. I've been waiting for you," the man called out. "Don't do anything dumb or the girl gets it."

Canyon made to reply while his eyes swept the trees and the thick foliage. But he saw nothing move.

"I want to talk, O'Grady. We can make a deal," Colbert called out.

"Where's your friend?" Canyon asked.

"Gone. He took off," Colbert said, and Canyon smiled. "He said he'd rather run than deal." Canyon kept silent, letting the minutes pass by, and he saw Colbert wipe one hand across his brow.

"You'll be getting more nervous, lad," Canyon whispered to himself.

"Dammit, O'Grady, come out where I can see you. We can make a deal. You let me walk away and you can have the girl," Colbert said. "You try to take me, and she's dead."

Canyon stayed motionless, his eyes moving across the circle of dense foliage again. He saw nothing, but the other man was somewhere behind the leafy curtain, waiting for his chance. Canyon sat back and remained silent.

"Goddammit, O'Grady, you going to come out so we can talk?" Colbert shouted, nervous impatience in his voice.

Canyon remained silent and another five minutes passed.

"A deal, dammit. I'm offering you a deal. Her life for mine. What more do you want?" Colbert shouted.

Canyon leaned against the trunk of a blue beech, his muscles relaxed, but his eyes riveted on Hal Colbert. He saw the man wipe his brow again with the back of one hand, but he kept the gun pressed into Carla's neck. Canyon let the minutes go by.

"All right, I can wait," Colbert snarled. "Just remember that she's dead if you try anything."

Canyon nodded to himself. He believed Colbert. The man would pull the trigger, if only in nervous panic. But Canyon continued to stay silent while his gaze stayed riveted on Colbert. The man wasn't up to the pressures he had created for himself, not by experience, not by training, not by character. Canyon knew he would see what he waited for. He had only to be patient. The wait wasn't as long as he had expected, and as his gaze riveted on Colbert, he saw the man's eyes flick to the foliage for an instant. Colbert's eyes flicked to the trees again, pulled back to Carla, and nervously flicked up to the foliage again.

Canyon's smile was sheathed in ice. Hal Colbert's flicking glances went only to one place, the foliage at his right. But Canyon waited again. He had to be certain. Colbert's tongue came out to lick across his dry lips, and his face twitched in nervousness. Again, his eyes flicked to the foliage on his right.

"This won't get you anywhere, O'Grady," Colbert called out. "That's the only deal I'm making." Again, the man's eyes went to the thick foliage at his right, then came back instantly.

But Canyon had seen enough now, and he rose, moved backward away from the tree trunk where Carla lay, the strain beginning to show on her face.

Canyon began to inch his way in a wide circle

through the trees. Silence was everything, he knew. Silence now and silence when he found his quarry. Anything else would mean Carla's life. He crawled, moved forward on his belly, a few inches at a time. He made a wide circle until he was finally to the right of where Colbert waited with Carla. With painstaking slowness, O'Grady began to move forward again, this time in a straight line. He heard Colbert call out again, the hint of a quaver in his voice.

"Y'know, I can get tired waiting. I can just blow her head off and you won't have any deal. You want that, O'Grady?" the man shouted.

Colbert's nerves were reaching the thin line, Canyon could hear. The man had been prepared for treachery, and if that failed, to use Carla as his ticket to get away. He hadn't prepared for silence. They seldom did, Canyon murmured inwardly. Silence was a tool and a weapon of awesome power. But his musings snapped off as he spied the figure crouched behind the thick foliage. The man held a heavy old Hawkens rifle in his hands, and his concentration was on Colbert, Carla, and the area in front of the fallen tree trunk.

Canyon inched forward again, heard Colbert shouting, and nodded in satisfaction. The man in front of him had his eyes and ears fixed on Colbert and the trees closest to him. He never heard his attacker reach him from behind, but he felt the pressure against his throat, so swift and so deadly he had time only to open his mouth in a soundless cry.

Canyon continued to squeeze. He couldn't afford to do less, and in moments the figure went limp and sank noiselessly to the ground. Canyon rose, unseen behind the curtain of thick foliage, but he saw Colbert's eyes flick to the leaves in front of him. He backed away and began to move on in the half-circle that would bring him behind Colbert. He moved silently, but without the need to be as completely silent as before.

Colbert was not close enough to hear the rustle of a leaf or the pressure of a footstep on a twig. He could move more quickly, and when he halted, he was in back of Colbert, still behind the heavy foliage.

Canyon's eyes narrowed as he saw Colbert's finger on the trigger of the gun pressed into Carla's neck. Even if a bullet plowed into the man, his finger could still tighten on the trigger, a reaction of nerves and muscles that needed no orders from the mind. But the result would be as deadly to Carla as if Colbert had done it deliberately.

Canyon's lips thinned. He had to find a way to get the six-gun away from Carla's neck. He frowned into space, cast aside one possibility after the other, all for the same reason: none offered enough safety margin for Carla. He was still wrestling with the dilemma when he heard the hoofbeats racing toward him. He yanked the Colt out, felt his brows lift as he saw the horse and rider race to a halt and Glenda leap to the ground. The trickle of blood was still on the side of her mouth, and she held the rifle in her hands.

"Get away from here, dammit," Colbert

yelled at her, but Glenda raised the rifle and aimed it at Carla.

"After I kill her," she said.

"No," Colbert screamed, and half-rose. "She's my ticket out of here. No, stop that, you crazy bitch."

"She's mine," Glenda screamed back, lifted the rifle another half-inch, and Canyon saw Colbert fire his six-gun, two shots that smashed into Glenda a split second before she pulled the trigger on the rifle. She staggered backward, the rifle dropping from her hands, her mouth falling open. She half-turned away as she collapsed to the ground, as if she'd found the strength to turn her back on Carla for the last time.

But Colbert was still standing with the six-gun in his hand. Canyon burst through the foliage. "Back here, Colbert," he yelled. The man whirled, tried to bring his gun up to fire when the Colt barked and Hal Colbert flew back to land draped across the fallen tree on his back.

Canyon holstered the Colt as he ran to Carla and pulled the rope from around her. She fell into his arms, clung to him with a terrible desperation, and he held her until the half-crying, half-sobbing sounds finally subsided. He lifted her to her feet and walked to the palomino with her. She leaned back against him in the saddle as he slowly rode away, and she listened to him as he told her everything that had happened.

She stared up at him when he finished. "It's unbelievable," she breathed. "Absolutely unbelievable."

"Only it happened, every twist and turn of it," he said. "They almost pulled it off, too. I'll tell it to your father when we get back."

"What happens now?" she asked.

"The election will go on. Your father will win, and in time, those who didn't vote for him will learn the truth of what happened. It'll take a little time to circulate, but it'll be heard."

She rode in silence with him, letting the magnitude of everything that had happened sink in. When he reached the ranch, she slid from the horse as Roy Gannet raced from the house. "I'll tell you all of it," she said to her father, and cast a glance at Canyon.

"Maybe that would be best," he agreed. "I'll fill in the details when I come back."

He left her walking slowly into the house with her father, and he rode into Dry Corn and took a room at the inn. "You won't be having any more problems," he said to the elderly desk clerk, and he smiled inwardly at the relief that flooded the man's face.

Canyon pulled the shade down in the little room, undressed, stretched out on the bed, and let himself enjoy the rewards of a deep sleep.

The day was nearing an end when he woke, washed, and dressed and stopped at the stage depot. He took a sheet of paper the depot provided and addressed the envelope first.

President James Buchanan
The White House
Washington, D.C.
USA

The message on the sheet of paper was but a few terse lines: "You were backing the wrong horse. Situation corrected. Details when I get back. Canyon O'Grady, Federal Agent."

He sealed the envelope and gave it to the depot master. It'd reach Washington before he did, he knew. He didn't plan a hurried trip back. He took Cormac from town and made his way back to the Gannet ranch, night covering the land when he reached it.

Carla opened the door of the main house as he dismounted and he saw she wore a white dressing robe, the onyx hair a striking contrast to it.

"Father's gone to Glenda's place," she said, and Canyon's brows lifted in surprise. "He's going to bring those horses of hers back here tomorrow," Carla explained. "Some good ought to come out of all this."

"Yes, that'd be nice," Canyon agreed, and followed Carla as she walked down the corridor to her room.

"He also fired Owen Dunstan," she said. "He wants to start things over here differently, especially if he's going to be the new senator."

"Good idea," Canyon said, and saw Carla study him, her head cocked to one side, a small smile edging her lips.

"Federal Agent Canyon O'Grady," she murmured. "That explains the charming role of tinker and wanderer. It doesn't explain or excuse some of the rest."

"Such as?" he asked mildly.

"Hopping into bed with Glenda," Carla said, her black eyes flashing at once.

"Oh, but it does," Canyon said. "That was in the line of duty."

"You expect me to believe that?"

"I do," he said.

"Even if it's not true?"

"That doesn't matter."

"Why not?"

"Because the only thing that matters is that you want to believe it," he said. "Things are to us as we perceive them to be. You want to believe it was in the line of duty, don't you?"

"Yes, damn you," Carla murmured.

"Then it was," he said. "Simple."

She reached up, pulled a tiny string, and the dressing gown parted and fell to the floor. "I'll show you simple," Carla murmured as she pressed her breasts against him.

"Simple and natural. I like that," Canyon said as he lay down on the bed with her. He was glad he'd sent the message to Washington. It could take him longer than he'd expected to get back.

KEEP A LOOKOUT!

The following is the opening section from the next novel in the action-packed new Signet Western series CANYON O'GRADY

CANYON O'GRADY # 5

THE LINCOLN ASSIGNMENT

August 1858, on the Illinois prairie, where the life of a man—and the future of an entire nation—depends on a quick wit and a straight shot

President James Buchanan leaned back in the big leather chair behind his massive desk and sighed. He was 67 years old and felt the full and massive weight and responsibility of being President smashing down on his narrow shoulders. He'd held the office for two years and it seemed right then like twenty.

He wiped a hand over his face and stared at the man across the desk from him.

"Canyon O'Grady. I know you usually take on more exciting jobs than this one, but this could turn out to be of vital importance to our nation. You know, we're having an election in two years.

"Already the candidates are lining up for the

job. I'm not running again. I believe in the democratic process. Let the people speak. We are a government by the people and for the people. And I damn well don't like the idea of seeing the deck stacked in anyone's favor, especially the Republicans.''

O'Grady, attired in his best black suit and string tie, sat on the edge of the chair, his back ramrod straight, his flame-red hair cut neatly for a change. He didn't have the slightest idea where the President was going with this line of talk.

Buchanan continued, ''We've been hearing rumors for weeks, and at last we have some concrete evidence, and some idea of what is going on. I fear that there is a plot afoot to limit the ballot for president, perhaps stack it in favor of one or the other of the parties. I won't stand for that.

''We're afraid the target is Senator Stephen A. Douglas, of Illinois. He's one of the leading Democratic candidates. Reports indicate that a team of deadly assassins is after the Senator.''

''Do we have any names, descriptions?'' asked O'Grady.

''Yes, we do. I'll turn you over to my assistant, Jamiston Priestly, who will be your contact and give you the details. I just want to be sure you understand how seriously I take this mission. We could be dealing with history here. If we don't catch the assassins and Douglas is killed he could never become President and influence this great nation the way I'm sure that he would as my successor.''

"Yes, Mr. President, I understand."

"I hope you do, Mr. O'Grady. I'm not out to protect only Senator Douglas even if he is from my party. This other fellow, his opponent Lincoln, is said to be coming up fast as a Republican candidate for the presidential nomination. Of course, I want you to put an end to this threat by jailing or eliminating the terrorizers. That way we'll be protecting both the possible presidential candidates."

The President peaked his fingers and stared over them.

"Now, Mr. O'Grady, if you have any more questions, I'm sure Mr. Priestly can take care of them."

O'Grady stood. "Thank you, Mr. President."

President Buchanan looked up, the fatigue evident in his eyes. O'Grady knew the man was feeling his age now and sagging under the pressures of the job.

"Stop them, O'Grady," Buchanan ordered. "Stop the bastards."

27 million Americans can't read a bedtime story to a child.

It's because 27 million adults in this country simply can't read.

Functional illiteracy has reached one out of five Americans. It robs them of even the simplest of human pleasures, like reading a fairy tale to a child.

You can change all this by joining the fight against illiteracy.

Call the Coalition for Literacy at toll-free **1-800-228-8813** and volunteer.

Volunteer Against Illiteracy. The only degree you need is a degree of caring.